DRAGON RIDERS
of
OSNEN

OTHER BOOKS

Bound by Blood

Chosen
Acolyte
Sworn

Marked by the Dragon

Curse of the Dragon
Scale of the Dragon
Egg of the Dragon
Call of the Dragon
Wrath of the Dragon

The Fallen King Chronicles

Dragonsphere
The Fallen King
The Valiant King
The Restored King

Dragons of Isentol

Throne of Deceit
Rune Marked
Empire of Serpents

Galactic Mercenaries

Steel for Hire
Steel for Free
Steel for All

DRAGON RIDERS OF OSNEN

RICHARD FIERCE

Dragon Riders of Osnen Omnibus 14-15
Copyright © 2025 by Richard Fierce

All rights reserved. This book or any portion thereof may not be reproduced, distributed, or transmitted in any form or by any means without the express written consent of the copyright holder, except in the case of brief quotations for the purpose of reviews and certain other noncommercial uses permitted by copyright law.

This is a work of fiction. All events portrayed in this book are fictitious, and any resemblance to real people or events is purely coincidental. All rights reserved, including the right to reproduce this book or portions thereof in any form without the express permission of the publisher.

Cover design by germancreative

Dragonfire Press

Print ISBN: 979-8-89631-051-8

First Edition: 2025

Wrath
and
Ruin

You lied to me.

Sion's words burned in my mind like a brand, and guilt assailed me.

I'm sorry, I said. *I thought I was doing what was best.*

Sion snorted. *Being deceitful is never what is best.*

Didn't you tell me to lie to the wild dragons about Drakus?

I told you we should kill him. I never told you to lie about it.

I thought back to our conversation and realized she was right. The path I found myself on seemed to grow darker with each decision I made. What was I doing? I ground my teeth in frustration.

I'm sorry, I repeated.

Never lie to me again.

I swallowed hard, nodding, and the silence stretched between us. She still didn't know about the orbs, but since they had been destroyed, I saw no point in telling her about them. She was already angry with me, and I didn't want to infuriate her further.

We rested atop a hill, and I stared off into the distance. The sun burned hot, heat waves dancing a slow dance, shimmering everything in sight. We had reached the mainland late last night, and the wild dragons were exhausted. Maren and Demris were with them, resting outside the port city. I felt like we were wasting valuable time, but I knew we couldn't push the poor dragons any harder.

Do you think the Citadel is still standing? I asked.

Master Anesko is a wise leader. I am sure he is keeping the king at bay.

I hoped that was true, though it was impossible to know for certain.

How long before they'll be ready to fly again?

Sion hummed softly, the sound vibrating the ground beneath me.

Give them a few hours. We can still reach the Citadel before nightfall.

I stood up and stretched. *I'll be back.*

Where are you going?

For a walk.

I strode down the hill, and I could feel Sion's confusion filtering through the bond. I didn't blame her. The way things were going recently had me confused as well. In trying to do what I thought was best, I continued to stumble. Perhaps it was best if I didn't try to play leader. Clearly, I was failing miserably at it. And despite that, Sion and Maren continued to follow me … but why?

I reached the bottom of the hill and breathed in deeply of the air. The smell of salt water still permeated my nostrils, but the moist earthy scent of the grass did well to drive it away. I enjoyed being out at sea, but it was good to be home. An invisible heaviness overcame me, and I paused to glance around.

"Eldwin."

My eyes blurred momentarily, and then I saw a cloaked figure standing before me. Instinctively, I put my hand on the hilt of my blade.

"I see you found the Wild Ones."

It was Tyrval.

I let go of the hilt and nodded, suddenly feeling exhausted. "Yes, we did. It would have been helpful to know your brother was playing god over them."

"Drakus is still alive? I'm impressed."

"He was," I clarified. "The Wild Ones took their wrath out on him."

Tyrval didn't seem fazed by the news. She probably hadn't seen him since he'd left the mainland, which was long enough to lose any familial connection.

"After they've rested, we're flying to the Citadel."

"Good," Tyrval replied. "When that is settled, the Assembly could use some help."

"With what?"

"We still haven't found Risod. Nemryth suspects the dragon slayers have captured her."

"My hands are full," I said. "I don't know how long it will take to deal with the king, and there's no guarantee we will be victorious."

"Dark times indeed, but we must never lose hope, my boy. The night is darkest before the dawn, as the saying goes."

I had never heard that saying before. If Tyrval thought it would inspire me, she was wrong.

"Send word if you find her," I said. "Otherwise, I will seek you out later."

With a blink of my eyes, Tyrval was gone. The heaviness I felt dissipated, and I stared at the spot where she had been. Had the Assembly not asked enough of me? There were many people in this world, and yet they always requested my aid. It was enough to drive me mad.

What's wrong? Sion's voice interrupted my thoughts.

What isn't? I replied. *Everyone in this world needs help and there aren't enough people to stand in the gap.*

My words took Sion by surprise. I felt her shock for only a moment before she recovered and withdrew from my mind. I stared off in the Citadel's direction and wondered what was next. It seemed as though there was always another battle to fight, as if there was never a moment of rest before something bad threatened the world. I heaved a sigh and trudged back up the hill to where Sion waited.

Forgive me, I said as I crouched in front of her. She blinked at me, and I ran my hand along her snout comfortingly. *I'm in a bad mood. Maybe with some sleep, I'll be back to myself again.*

There is more to your brooding than lack of rest. Darkness weighs on your heart. I can feel it in our bond.

I wanted to argue with her, but I knew she was right. Ever since T'Mere's death, the suffocating weight of death and despair had slowly been clawing its way into my mind. I ignored it by focusing on everything else, and perhaps that was the reason I continued to fail. Yet if I faced the darkness, would I defeat it, or be lost to it?

None of us are perfect creations, Sion said.

Not even dragons? I asked, cracking a slight grin.

Not even dragons.

An overwhelming rush of emotions hit me suddenly, and it took every ounce of strength to keep the tears from falling. What kind of leader cried when things got difficult? I closed my eyes and rested my forehead against Sion's hard scales.

You will survive this, she said.

How do you know?

Because I will flame your soul from the afterlife if you do not.

That made me laugh, and this time, I did not stop the tears from coming. I wrapped my arms around Sion's massive head and held onto her as tightly as I could, as if she alone could stop my descent into madness.

After a long moment, I released her and wiped the tears from my cheeks. It dawned on me that the world was much like the Path on the Island of Lost Souls. It demanded much and gave little in return, but if I had survived that terrible place, I could certainly survive this ordeal.

Thank you for never giving up on me, I said.

Sion nuzzled me, knocking me over backward. *Dragons never give up.*

That is a good thing.

Indeed. A war is coming, and dragons will decide the fate of the Order.

And of Osnen, I said solemnly.

THERE WAS NOTHING THAT BURNED hotter than dragon fire.

Tents and grass were consumed and stones melted as Sion breathed her flames across the small camp of royal scouts. The soldiers died silently, taken completely by surprise. I shielded my face from the heat and held my breath until Sion swooped up and the air grew cooler. The devastation made me glad I had never been at the wrong end of a dragon's wrath.

I'm surprised Erling has scouts this far west. The Citadel is still miles away.

Perhaps he thinks more riders coming to aid Anesko? Sion suggested.

Maybe, but he knows our numbers are limited. Unless a spy informed him of our plan to find the wild dragons, I doubt he's expecting a surprise.

Sion wheeled in a wide circle, and I scanned the ground for more scouts.

All looks clear to me.

If there are scouts out here, I think they will be closer to the Citadel, Sion said. *How will we get inside without notice?*

I'd spent a lot of time thinking about that, and I'd decided on a path that was likely a suicide mission. I sent an image of what I was considering through the bond and waited for Sion to rebuke me. Surprisingly, she seemed pleased with the idea.

It is full of risk, but it is the last thing anyone will expect.

That was my thought as well, I said. *We just need everyone to agree. My only fear is these dragons don't have any battle experience. They're likely to cause more damage than help.*

That is possible, Sion agreed. *But the only ones outside the safety of the Citadel are the king's men. I say bring on the destruction.*

I smiled and patted her neck. Sion turned back the way we came and flew until the wild dragons came into view. She landed near Demris, and I dismounted and slid down Sion's shoulder, then trudged to where Maren was sitting. She looked up as I approached.

"The scouts have been dealt with," I said.

"Good. The way ahead should be clear, then?"

"I'm not sure. Sion thinks there may be more the closer we get. I could take the lead and make sure, but if we're spotted, then we'll lose the element of surprise."

"If there are enough scouts, we'll be discovered, regardless."

"I know, but I have a plan."

Maren stared at me expectantly.

"Instead of trying to get into the Citadel, I think we should strike at your father's forces."

Just as I expected with Sion, I assumed she would argue against my idea. Instead, she nodded.

"Surprise them."

"Exactly," I said.

"It's risky."

"If we cause enough chaos, they'll retreat. That will give us the opportunity we need to get inside the Citadel without risking everyone else's safety."

"What if they don't retreat?" Maren asked.

"If they are wise, they will," I replied. "Otherwise, their losses will be heavy."

"If I know my father, he'll have his best men closest to the Citadel. They won't flee at the first sign of trouble."

"Nobody said this was going to be easy. Besides, if we succeed, we'll be trapped inside the school, but I can't think of anything better."

Maren nodded. "Once all our forces are pooled together, we can decide what to do next. It's settled, then. Now we just have to convince Getarros."

Getarros hadn't spoken to me since we'd arrived. I was certain his rage still burned hot, but without him and the other wild dragons, we didn't stand a chance against the king.

"Any ideas on what I should say?" I asked.

"I'll speak to him, but you need to be with me. He may be angry with you, but he has no reason not to follow you. If it wasn't for you, he would still be a slave to Drakus."

Maren had a point, but dragons were stubborn creatures. If he decided he no longer trusted me, there was nothing she could do to sway him.

"Let's get it over with, then."

I helped Maren to her feet, and we strode across the grassy field to where Getarros lay. The dragon was basking in the sun. He opened his eyes as we advanced, and his tail flicked back and forth in an agitated manner. He yawned as he rose to his feet, a deep growl rumbling in his chest.

"We need to speak with you," Maren said.

Getarros turned his gaze on me, and the tension was as thick as smoke. Despite the fear he instilled in me, I kept my eyes locked on his. He looked at Maren, and the two must have started talking. I reached out to Getarros, but he'd blocked me from his mind. After a long moment of awkward silence, Maren looked at me.

"He wants to speak with you."

I nodded hesitantly. I didn't think he would do anything to harm me, but I let Sion know anyway. Maren kissed me on the cheek and walked away, leaving the two of us alone.

If you are still angry with me, I understand. I am angry with myself.

I am not one to brood over past mistakes, Getarros replied.

Relief washed over me.

You seem to be avoiding me, so I assumed—

It is not you that troubles my thoughts. All my life, I have served Drakus. Now that he is gone, there is a void that hangs over me, over all my brethren. At the Whispering Cliffs, we knew our place. We do not know our place here in your land.

His words surprised me. It sounded as if he was afraid. A dragon, afraid? It was a strange thought.

Master Anesko at the Citadel will welcome you and the others. All the riders will.

I do not doubt that, but your hospitality is not what burdens me. We are not like Sion and Demris.

Getarros looked past me at Sion for a moment.

We do not want to bond with humans, he said.

My hopes of restoring the Order to its full glory crashed, shattering like a thousand pieces of glass.

I don't understand.

I don't expect you to.

Silence stretched between us, and I swallowed the lump that had formed in my throat.

Without you, we cannot defeat the king.

Yes, I have already considered this. We will help you with your battle, but when it is done, we will leave and make our own place in this new world.

That was a sliver of hope, at least.

You and your brethren are the hope of future generations. Without you to strengthen the Order, it is unlikely we will survive. Once the riders are gone, there will be no one to protect the land from tyrants like the king.

Where there is evil, good will always rise to meet it, Getarros said.

Will you at least reconsider?

No, I have made up my mind on this matter.

That was it, then. There was no way to force them to bond with humans. For a brief moment, I wished we still had the orbs. I immediately pushed the thought away and berated myself for even thinking that. Even if we did still have the orbs, I could never use them in good conscience, not to force the dragons into a second slavery.

Very well. I will not press the issue. It is more than enough that you are going to help us.

Indeed, it is more than you deserve.

I thought you weren't still angry? I asked.

I'm not, but you have caused more pain than you know. My brethren and I must now learn to do many things. To hunt, to defend ourselves. We did not have these worries under Drakus. You may have freed us from a tyrant, but now we are prisoners to ignorance.

I had not considered that, but I had not considered the dragons would not join the Order, either. The number of mistakes I made continued to grow. Even if we saved Osnen from the king, it seemed the Order was doomed to die out.

MAREN AND I SAT TOGETHER among the tall grass, daylight long gone. A small fire burned low, the flames dancing with vigor as if all in the world was well. The slumbering of the wild dragons filled the air, the sound like that of a strong wind.

"We have failed," I whispered.

"How so?" Maren asked, turning her head to look at me.

"If Getarros and the others will not bond with humans, then the riders will end. We are too few as it is. If Anesko was contemplating disbanding us before, he will certainly consider it again now."

Maren rested her head on my shoulder. "You worry too much."

"How can I not? And how can you be so calm about things?"

"I have faith things will work out in the end."

I laughed, but not out of humor. "Your faith is stronger than mine."

"I do worry about the future, Eldwin. I just try not to dwell on things I cannot control. We will survive whatever comes our way, good or ill."

The fire crackled, and a small flame leaped from the coals, temporarily lighting the shadows. The darkness was deep this night, and it reminded me of the feeling I experienced when Sion had been cut off from me on the Island of Lost Souls. I had seen many terrible things since then, but I always persevered. Perhaps Maren's faith was not unfounded.

"I'm going to bed," she said, lifting her head off me. "Tomorrow will be difficult enough, even with plenty of sleep."

I nodded absently, still lost in my thoughts. Maren wandered over to Demris and curled up beside him. The air wasn't chill, but the warmth of a dragon was always comforting. I leaned back on my elbows and stared up at the moon.

As a child, I had dreamed of becoming a dragon rider, following in my father's steps. He had taught me about honor and love, but nothing about dragons or the school. I still found that odd. Had he wanted me to learn things on my own, or protect me from living the same harsh life he had?

Silence your thoughts, Sion's voice rumbled in my mind. *I cannot sleep with your constant worries.*

Sorry, I replied. *I can't help it.*

I closed the bond on my end and continued to stare at the moon. It was little more than half full. Perhaps my father's silence on the latter things was indeed because he wanted to protect me. That made me a fool, then. Not only a fool, but arrogant and selfish.

Again, my mind strayed to the coming battle. How could we defeat a king? A man so confident in his own power, he had no qualms about destroying the very people who protected his kingdom.

I sighed. It was impossible to ignore my anxious thoughts. Staring at the moon certainly wasn't helping. I stood up and walked along the field toward a small stream I had seen earlier. Perhaps drowning myself in cold water would take my mind off things. I knelt in front of the water and was about to put my hands in when I abruptly stopped and froze.

I sensed something, but I didn't know what it was. Glancing around revealed nothing but the shadowy swaying of the grass. I reopened the bond.

Sion?

I am here.

Do you sense anything out of the ordinary?

There was a pause, and I heard her stirring across the way.

Magic, she said. *I think it's the dragon slayers.*

I recoiled from the stream and drew my sword, shifting my gaze back and forth. I thought she had killed the sorcerer. Did the other slayers know magic as well? A few moments passed and nothing happened. Sion joined me near the stream and sniffed the air.

Whoever it was is gone now, she said.

You said it might be the dragon slayers. Do you think it could have been a scout from the king's army?

No. The feel of the magic was the same as the slayers.

We stood guard until I grew too tired to stay alert. I sheathed my blade and followed Sion back to the camp. She got comfortable, and I lay beside her.

I can barely keep my eyes open, I said.

Rest. I will keep watch.

I fell asleep and was greeted by bad dreams about dragon slayers, the fall of the Order, and the king terrorizing Osnen. When dawn came, I awoke to find many of the dragons ready to go, eager even. Maren had prepared breakfast, and I devoured my portion quickly. Despite my fears, there was a level of excitement about returning to the Citadel. It was the only home I had, after all.

Once all the dragons were ready, we flew for the Citadel. Unlike the many other times I had returned to the school, this time felt like a march to war. There was a mixture of fear and determination in the air, and it put me on edge. Sion kept a close eye on the ground, watching for scouts, but fortune was on our side as the way was clear.

Things may actually go according to plan, I told Sion.

That would be a welcome change.

Indeed.

As we drew closer to the Citadel, plumes of smoke rose in the distance. At first, I thought the school was burning, but I soon realized it was only the fires from the king's encampment. Demris and Maren flew to our right, and I looked over, catching Maren's attention.

"Get ready!" I shouted into the wind.

She nodded, her expression serious. I mouthed the words 'I love you.' She smiled and mouthed them back, and I turned my attention ahead. There were countless tents outside the walls of the school, and the camp took up several acres. Soldiers were everywhere, numbering in the thousands. Banners with the royal crest fluttered from poles, and we descended toward the nearest tents.

A horn blared as someone spotted us, and the king's riders took to the air to meet us. Roars of challenge rang out, and I looked over my shoulder to see the wild dragons break formation into smaller groups. They split up and descended upon the camp, breathing fire and smashing things with their tails.

Considering their lack of experience, their display impressed me. A small group of the king's riders ignored them and came straight for me and Maren.

Brace yourself, Sion warned.

She spun in a circle to the left and engaged a blue dragon. The soldier on its back held a lance at the ready, the tip of the weapon gleaming under the sun. At the last moment, Sion stretched her wings out, catching the air. Her upper body lifted, sending her rear claws into the face of the other dragon. A sharp sound tore through the air as her claws scraped against the enemy's scales.

I flinched and covered my ears, gripping the saddle tight with my legs. The other dragon roared and maneuvered away from Sion, lashing at her with its tail. Sion gave chase, following the beast as it winged its way around the protective shield of the Citadel. The soldier was a skilled rider, guiding his mount left and right to avoid the blasts of flame that Sion breathed at them.

The wind whipped through my hair with every twist and turn and dried my eyes out to the point I had to shield my face in the crook of my elbow. The smell of smoke and brimstone hit my nostrils, and I risked a glance down at the encampment to see what damage the dragons had done.

A third of the camp was on fire, but the progress of the wild dragons was now stalled as they began battling the king's riders. The organization they had displayed initially was gone, replaced by chaos as their ranks broke. I watched in horror as several of the dragons were slaughtered brutally, their bodies falling from the sky and crashing among the camp.

Sion roared in surprise, and I looked up. Half a dozen royal riders came rushing toward us. The blue dragon had lured us into a trap.

THE RIDERS FLEW IN A tight formation, their wings stretched wide to form a wall that blocked the way forward. I looked around desperately, searching for a way to escape. My heart was racing, and my mind was spinning with possibilities. We could fly straight up, but they would certainly follow us. Then I saw a gap between two riders on the right side of their formation.

It was small, but if we could get through it, then maybe we could break away from them and regroup with Demris and Maren. I risked a glance in the direction they had been, but I could no longer see them.

Can you make it? I asked, sending Sion a mental image.

I will try.

She lashed her tail with determination and flew straight for the gap. The royal riders must have seen what we were doing because they moved faster to box us in even as we approached. I gritted my teeth as I watched the riders surge toward us.

The riders pinned us down, closing in on all sides, leaving us with no way out. We were outnumbered and outmatched, and there was no way we could fight our way out of this one and survive.

A shadow passed overhead, and a moment later, Getarros and a group of wild dragons swooped in from above. Their sudden arrival caught the royal riders off guard, giving Sion an opening to make her escape. I urged her on, and she flew up as fast as she could. The wind rushed past my ears as we soared higher and higher into the sky, putting distance between us and the king's soldiers.

The sun shone brightly, its rays illuminating everything below us in a golden hue. Looking down, I could see the king's soldiers and the wild dragons battling. Getarros's group had the advantage, and they were slowly driving the royal riders back.

They are holding their own well, I said.

Yes, but if the king's men coordinate their efforts, we will lose the advantage. We need to do something to force them into a retreat. It would not be wise for Anesko to lower the shield with the enemy this close to the walls.

She was right. I scanned the encampment below. The ranks of the wild dragons had broken, the beasts scattered and struggling. It was a very different sight than watching Getarros and his group as they took down the royal riders.

We need to rally them, I said. *Then flame the camp all the way to the king's tent.*

Shouldn't we target the king directly? That will end things quickly.

Not unless Maren is with us. It won't be that easy to get rid of the king. I'm sure he's got sorcerers nearby.

I'll flame them, too, Sion growled.

I don't doubt you would. Let's get the attention of the wild dragons. We need to bring the heat.

Sion dove, rushing past Getarros's group, and issued an ear-splitting roar as she arced over the camp. Half a dozen dragons looked at her and winged their way to our side. Sion flew back and forth over the camp, and with each pass, more dragons answered her call, including Demis. Maren nodded at me, and I was glad to see they were safe. The royal riders broke away from the battle and pulled back, surrounding the king's pavilion.

It's working, I said. *The king must be worried.*

They are regrouping. Many of the wild ones have fallen, and while we still have numbers on our side, our enemy outmatches us in experience.

I surveyed the camp again now that we were closer to the ground and saw the terrible truth of her words. Roughly a third of the wild dragons were dead or mortally wounded. The pained cries of men and beasts filled the air, and I knew that no matter how this battle ended, there truly was no victor.

We need to attack them now, before they recover.

As you command, Sion replied.

She roared and changed direction, heading toward the royal riders. The wild dragons flew with us, and as we converged on the king's tent, the world erupted in fire and heat. Archers were positioned around the tent, and volleys of arrows filled the sky. The attack served no purpose, at least none that I could discern, and the projectiles clinked harmlessly off the dragons' scales.

Sion breathed a torrent of flames into their ranks, and the smell of burning wood, metal, and flesh seared my nostrils. The king's pavilion, however, remained untouched. The flames that came within a few feet were immediately snuffed out.

You were right, Sion said. *The king's sorcerers are protecting him.*

We can do nothing about that, but we can drive his riders away.

"Ignore the soldiers on the ground!" I shouted. "Attack the riders!"

More arrows sailed through the air, but Sion and the other dragons were undeterred. She opened her jaws and bathed our enemies in the orange glow of her flames. The heat was suffocating, and I did my best to hide behind Sion's bulk until it was safe.

When I looked up, my hopes soared. The royal riders were retreating, leaving the king's pavilion behind. A chorus of roars arose from the wild dragons, and Sion and Demris joined their celebratory sounds.

This is only a minor victory, I said. *Now we must hurry to the Citadel.*

Let them be proud. They are not warriors like us.

Sion circled back and flew for the Citadel. The magical shield was still up, and as we got closer, I saw a line of people on the wall. Anesko's robed form was unmistakable. I waved at him, and a moment later, the shield flickered out of existence. I looked over my shoulder and motioned for the wild dragons to fly ahead.

They continued onward, and Sion and I remained outside the walls. I kept my eyes on the king's camp, but the royal riders had not returned yet. Once all the dragons were safely inside the confines of the Citadel, we crossed over the wall and landed in the crowded courtyard. I dismounted and hurried to meet Anesko as he purposely bounded down the stairs from the ramparts.

"You found them," he said breathlessly.

"We did, but it wasn't easy."

"You do not know how glad I am to see you." He stared past me. "There are so many of them."

"There were more, but we lost a lot of them in the battle. It was the only way I could think to clear a way into the Citadel."

"You were forced to make a difficult choice," Anesko said. "In your shoes, I would have chosen the same path. The risk was great, but it paid off."

"Yes, but now we are prisoners inside our own home."

"I am confident we will find a way out of this. Now that you have returned, we will convene with the other Curates and decide on a plan of action." Anesko frowned and turned his attention from the wild dragons to me. "They look malnourished."

I nodded. "It's a long story."

"Walk with me. I want to know everything."

MASTER ANESKO STOOD AT THE end of the table in the assembly room. He looked tired, and a myriad of red lines filled the whites of his eyes. Despite his obvious exhaustion, his demeanor was full of confidence, though I assumed it was a façade. I did not envy his position.

Maren sat on my left, and Katori was on my right. I finally felt at home again, but the feeling was tainted. I also knew the Citadel might not be our home much longer, depending on how things went. Anesko clasped his hands behind his back and cleared his throat, pulling me from my reverie.

"I think we all know how dire our situation is. We are, quite literally, surrounded by enemies, and their numbers are greater than our own."

An uneasy murmur echoed throughout the chamber. Anesko raised a hand for silence.

"What of the wild dragons?" Curate Henrik asked. "They should bolster our numbers."

"They are helpful, but we don't have enough riders for them. And judging by what I saw, they are not trained to fight. I fear many more of them will fall before this is over."

"If I may?" I said, standing up.

Anesko nodded.

"These dragons have been through a lot, and they chose to come here to help us. But they do not plan on staying after this fight is over. They will leave and find a place to call their own. I know that is not what any of us wanted to hear, but I felt it prudent to mention before we decide on any course of action."

"Thank you, Eldwin," Anesko said. "With that in mind, it begs a question each of us must answer. If we turn the tides in our favor, what does the future hold?"

A sinking feeling tugged at my stomach, and I took my seat. Was he considering disbanding the riders again? That would be foolish, especially if we defeated the king's army. There would be a void of power, and the riders would need to fill it.

"Is the future of the Order in question? Again?" It was Henrik, and it was almost as if he was speaking my thoughts. Perhaps everyone in the room had the same fear.

"I am only asking a question, my friend. If we win this war, what happens? Osnen will need a new ruler, not only to guide her, but to protect her. Look around this room. We are all that is left of the leadership. The Terranese school is gone, and we have heard nothing from Valgaard since the Assembly imprisoned Hrodin. We are short of both riders and dragons. We must look ourselves in the mirror and admit the Order is dying."

His words cut me to my very core, and they stung as sharp as any wound because they were true. I looked at Maren. Her eyes were watery with tears. I grabbed her hand, and she squeezed mine in response. As much as I wanted to disagree with Anesko, I knew he was right. The Order *was* dying, and there didn't seem to be any way to stop it.

"If there is no hope, then why fight at all?" I asked. "Why not let the shield down and open the gates?" My question was sincere, but the words spilled out of my mouth with anger and pain.

"I am not saying that we should surrender, to the king or to fate," Anesko replied gently. "I only want us all to be aware of the reality that faces us."

I ground my teeth in frustration. All of us knew the reality, but no one was trying to change it.

"We know there are many difficulties ahead, but that has never stopped us before. Instead of focusing on the problems, we should turn our attention to finding solutions. Let's deal with the problem at hand. We are prisoners here so long as the king is at our gates. How do we drive him back? If you have an idea, no matter how outlandish, speak it now."

"We could retreat to the Terranese school," Katori said. "The king would have to march his army far indeed to reach those gates. By the time they arrived, we would hold every advantage."

"I don't think that's wise," Anesko replied. "Other than yourself, none of us are familiar with those grounds. We'd be at a disadvantage, just as the king would. Besides, we would still have to figure out a way to escape without notice."

"We could call on the Assembly," I suggested.

"How would they help?"

I paused, as I didn't have an appropriate answer. They were also busy with the dragon slayers and trying to find Risod.

"I ... don't know," I said lamely.

Anesko looked around the table at each of us, but no other ideas were forthcoming. I leaned back in my seat and tried not to let the despair win. Maren and I had returned only to face our doom. Perhaps we should have stayed away from the Citadel and instead taken the wild dragons to a new home and started a new order.

Do not think of such things. Sion's voice lanced through my dark thoughts, scattering them.

I'm sorry. I didn't mean for them to overwhelm me like that.

A flood of comfort funneled through the bond, and despair was replaced with hope.

"My father will not stop until he has crushed the Order from existence," Maren said. "If we flee, he will follow us. We cannot run from this war. No, we must meet it head-on. We must strike him a direct blow."

Anesko turned his gaze to her. "How do you propose we do that? The lines of men between us and him are thick. Even if we were equal in number, the clash of arms would ruin both of our forces."

"We don't need to clash with his army to win. We just need to cut the head from the snake. If my father falls, chaos will consume the others. His generals will fight one another for power, giving us the perfect distraction to finish them off or force them to surrender."

"We tried that already," I said. "We reached his tent and his sorcerers protected him."

"That is because they saw us coming."

"What are you thinking?" Anesko asked. "That we should cloak our movements?"

Maren shook her head. "No. Even if we could generate enough magic to hide our forces, his sorcerers would sense our spells before we could get close enough to do anything. What I propose is something else."

She paused for a moment, and I stared at her intently, wondering what she had come up with.

"We should send someone to kill him."

"An assassin?" Anesko asked. "We are warriors, not killers."

"In this case, we must be both. The one who goes will need to do so alone and without magic. What better way to hide than in plain sight?"

That was so simple, and yet so brilliant. And I knew immediately that it should be me. This had all started because the king wanted me, and that meant it would have to end with me.

"Under normal circumstances, I would never agree with such measures." Anesko sighed and rubbed his eyes. "But the situation we find ourselves in is far from normal. Whoever accepts this task may not be successful, and knowing the king, he will kill the one who fails. I do not think we should leave this to just any rider. It should be one of us in this room."

I nodded in agreement.

"Who will volunteer to kill the king?"

Before I could answer, Maren rose from her chair.

"There is no need for anyone to volunteer. I will do it."

6

"You cannot do this," I said.

"I should be the one to do it. He is my father, after all."

Anesko had dismissed the others and left, leaving Maren and me alone at the table.

"How will you get through the camp if you don't plan on using your magic?"

"I will disguise myself as one of his soldiers," she said simply.

"What if you get caught?"

"What if I don't?"

I knew arguing with her was pointless, but I couldn't let her risk her life. She would feel the same way if I went, so ultimately there was no way either of us could win this debate.

"I fear losing you," I whispered.

Maren slid her chair closer and leaned against me. I embraced her tightly.

"I'll be as safe as I can. I will kill him and come straight back here."

I had learned long ago there was no talking her out of something once she'd made up her mind, and I didn't plan on arguing with her anymore. No, instead, I would have to find a way to keep her from leaving the Citadel.

"You should probably go when it's dark," I said. "Are you going to tell Demris?"

"No. Please don't let Sion say anything to him."

I nodded. Maren smiled and planted a kiss on my lips, then stood up.

"Make sure you're part of the distraction Anesko has in mind, just in case something happens."

"I'll be there."

Maren left the room, and I stared at the wall absently, mulling over how I could get her to stay. Aside from forcefully locking her up, I couldn't think of anything.

There is another way, Sion's voice interrupted my thoughts. *Though Maren will be angry with you if you employ it.*

What is it?

You could put her to sleep.

What do you mean?

Sion sent an image through the bond of a toothed silver-green stalk that bore a white flower. I'd never seen it before.

What is it?

It's a flower that can make a powder that causes drowsiness.

You want me to drug her? It surprised me Sion would even propose something like that.

I was only offering a suggestion to your dilemma, though I dislike the idea of you going to the camp alone.

It's not like you can go with me, and I don't want Maren being taken captive or killed by her father.

Sion rumbled, frustrated, but she had nothing else to say. I scratched an itch on my scalp and considered Sion's idea. She was right. Maren would be furious with me if I drugged her.

And yet ...

It would keep her safe in the Citadel. It was that or temporarily lock her in the dungeon. Neither option was ideal, but I felt as though the flower was the least of two evils. I left the chamber and traversed the halls. A Curate that died during Hrodin's treachery had tended a small garden, and I figured that would be the best place to check for the flower considering Surrel from the library had taken it over.

The door to the botanical room was propped open, and I saw Surrel was inside. She held a watering can and was pouring water into a large pot of yellow flowers. I knocked on the door frame and she looked up.

"Son of Matthias," she greeted.

I smiled at her. She was one of the first people I met when I arrived at the school, and she had always been kind to me.

"Hello, Surrel. I need something, and I thought you might be able to help."

"Of course."

"I'm looking for a certain plant. It grows a white flower."

A glance around the room revealed that wasn't the best description since there was a multitude of white flowers. Clematis, periwinkle, hyacinth, rhododendron, and a few others I didn't know the name of were scattered in pots all over the room.

"Do you know the name of this flower?" she asked.

"Uh, I don't." Sion sent me the image of it again. "It secretes a milky fluid when the seed pod is cut. Does that help?"

"Yes, that narrows it down precisely. I have to ask, what do you need it for? That milky substance is known to be addictive for those who abuse its use."

"I can't say, unfortunately," I replied. "Master Anesko and …" I waved a hand around, indicating the school.

"Ah, yes. For our enemies. I understand."

Surrel set the watering can down and walked over to a pot of flowers that sat atop a shelf in the back corner of the room. She unsheathed a small blade from her waist and went to work, drawing the milky fluid out of the seed pods.

"How do the plants grow in here with no sunlight?" I asked.

Surrel paused in her work to point at the globes of light that floated near the ceiling.

"Those were specifically designed to provide a light source as close to the sun as possible. They get the job done well, as you can see. How much of this stuff do you need?"

"Not much. Enough for one person should be sufficient."

She turned around and held out a glass vial. A small amount of thin pearly liquid sat at the bottom.

"You'll need to let it air dry, then crush it into a powder."

"Does it dissolve in water?"

"Yes, but I would suggest wine or tea, otherwise the taste is noticeable."

I took the vial and nodded.

"Thank you. As always, I appreciate your help."

"It is my pleasure, Son of Matthias."

"You know you can call me Eldwin," I said.

"I know." Surrel smiled and retrieved her watering can and resumed watering the flowers.

I clutched the vial in my hand and left. Maren didn't drink wine, so I would have to use tea to mask the powder. I went to our chambers and left the vial on the windowsill to allow the liquid to dry. Doubt tried to creep into my mind, but I ignored it. Maren would be angry, yes, but she would understand. At least, I hoped she would.

The rest of the day passed quickly, and by the time I returned to the room at dusk, the liquid had dried. I crushed the stuff into powder and hid the vial in my coin purse. At dinner, Maren and I sat at our usual table. My palms were sweating, and I had the feeling I was betraying her somehow.

I reminded myself why I was doing this. When Maren left the table for a moment, I poured the powder into her cup and quickly stirred it. She came back and took a drink. I prayed she wouldn't notice the taste. If she did, she said nothing.

The stuff must have been potent indeed, because it didn't take long for Maren to feel the effects of it. She moved sluggishly, and there were long pauses between her words.

"Are you feeling all right?" I asked.

"I'm not ... sure."

She stared off at nothing, but her facial expression made it seem like she was seeing something interesting.

"Maybe you should go to bed."

"That ... sounds great," Maren replied. "Wait. No. No, I can't. I have ... something important to do, but ... I can't remember what it is."

"I'm sure it'll come to you. Come on, I'll help you to bed. Some rest will do you some good."

She was unsteady on her feet and disoriented, and I again felt guilty for using the powder on her. I got her to our room and into the bed, and she passed out almost immediately.

It's done, I told Sion. *Now it's time to kill a king.*

7

I JOINED ANESKO ON THE parapet of the wall and stared down at the camp that stretched out in front of the Citadel.

"Where's Maren?"

The question was innocent, but it made me feel as though Anesko knew what I had done. I swallowed the lump in my throat.

"Change of plans," I said. "She's not feeling well and laid down to rest. I'm going instead."

Anesko gave me a questioning look, but nodded.

"Very well."

"Have you decided what the distraction will be?"

"It is too dangerous to send anyone outside the walls, so unless you are in trouble, there will not be one."

I creased my brow in concern.

"Are you sure that's the best idea?" I asked. "With the focus elsewhere, it will be easier for me to sneak through the camp."

"I am sure. We would have to bring the shield down to send riders out, opening ourselves up to an attack. The risk is too great, especially with the king's riders so close to the walls."

"I'm on my own, then?"

"Not quite," Anesko said. "If you get into trouble, use this."

He held up a war horn. I took it and turned it over in my hands, inspecting it. It was carved of wood and had runes engraved on the sides. Wrapped around the wider end of it was a leather thong.

"So I blow into this, and what happens?"

"It will alert me, but those around you will hear nothing. Only use it if you are in grave danger. I don't want to risk our safety for the sake of anything less than your possible death."

I slipped the thong onto my belt and adjusted the horn so it rested against my right hip. My sword was sheathed on the left side, and the combined weight tugged at my pants in an unbalanced manner.

"If you can't bring the shield down, how do I get out there?" I asked.

"I will open a small hole in the barrier. You'll have to be quick, though. It won't stay open long, and if it closes on you, it'll kill you."

"Of course it will. If something happens and I don't make it back, tell Maren I'm sorry."

"For what?"

"She'll know," I replied, casting another look at the camp. There was no reason to delay the inevitable. "I'm ready if you are."

Anesko nodded. "Come with me."

He led the way down the stairs to the courtyard, then followed the wall around to the eastern end of the Citadel.

"Where are we going?"

"To a secret door. It is rarely used and is only for emergencies, so do not reveal it to anyone else."

Anesko paused at a portion of the wall that didn't have any torches. He placed a hand on the stones and felt around.

"You don't know how to open it?" I asked.

"I do, but as I said, it is rarely used. Ah, yes, here it is."

He pushed one stone with both hands and it sank into the wall with a soft scraping sound. There was a moment of silence, and then a two-foot by three-foot section of the wall slid back a few inches before disappearing into the stones on the right.

"That's not a very big door," I said.

"You'll have to crawl through."

"I figured."

We stared at one another for a moment before Anesko laid a hand on my shoulder.

"Be careful, Eldwin. I expect to see you back here before dawn."

"I'm always careful." He gave me a stern look, and I smiled sheepishly. "I always *try* to be careful."

"Don't try. Just do it."

"Yes, sir."

I knelt on the ground and waited. Anesko muttered some words, and the barrier faded from the open section of the wall. I hastily crawled through the makeshift doorway, then stood and brushed my hands off on my pants. I turned to look at the doorway and saw the barrier was already whole again. The stones slid back into place, closing me off from the Citadel. That part was easy enough.

Do not get caught, Sion said.

I don't plan to.

We shall see.

Clouds filled the night sky, leaving little light to see by, but it was the perfect cover for me to make my way into the camp. I stepped lightly and kept my hand on the hilt of my blade, mostly to keep it from swinging about. As I drew close to the border of the camp, I could see it was heavily guarded, with a constant stream of soldiers patrolling the perimeter.

The glow of campfires illuminated the outline of tents and other structures, and I skulked ahead quietly. Getting past the patrols was going to pose a challenge, but I had an idea. I waited until a group of soldiers marched past, then I sprinted to the nearest tent and squatted down, keeping to the shadows.

My heart was hammering in my chest, but it was only partially from running. I was scared. No, terrified.

Calm yourself, Sion bade gently. *Stay alert.*

I nodded to myself, then took a few deep breaths. The footsteps of the next patrol drew close, and as they trudged past the opposite side of the tent, I stepped out from the shadows and joined them, walking at the rear of the group. None of them noticed me. I marched along with them until I spotted a row of tents that were backed up close to one another, providing an improvised path free from prying eyes.

I glanced over my shoulder and saw the next patrol was far enough away that they hopefully wouldn't see me break away. I counted silently in my head, and as we marched past the tents, I stepped into the shadows and hurried down the row. Fortune was with me, and again, no one noticed anything. I paused to get my bearings and peered between a gap in the tents to find the king's pavilion.

It's so much easier to find things from the sky, I complained to Sion.

Of course, it is. Are you having trouble?

A little. I'm not sure where to go.

Show me.

I sent an image of my surroundings through the bond.

You are on the northeast side of the camp. The king is in the center, so you'll need to go southwest. Move diagonally through the camp.

What would I do without you? I asked.

Probably die.

I snorted and couldn't help but smile. With a clear direction in mind, I made my way across the camp, pausing in the shadows and hiding behind tents when soldiers were nearby. Before long, I reached the king's pavilion. I crept along the backside and heard the faint sound of voices coming from within the tent. It was probably Erling and his advisors. I remained where I was and waited impatiently for their meeting to end, constantly checking my surroundings for soldiers.

After what felt like an hour, the voices faded. I waited a few moments more and carefully cut a slit in the tent with my sword. I would have climbed under, but the tent canvas was stretched too tight to lift the bottom. Peering inside, I saw Erling sitting in an elegant chair, his back to me. In front of the chair was a brazier that flickered with orange flames.

This is it.

I clenched my hand around the hilt of my blade and slipped into the tent, stepping lightly. A massive plush rug covered the ground, and it helped to mute my steps. A few strides brought me behind the chair, and I raised the blade above my head, ready to strike Erling a death blow. My muscles tensed, and just as I was about to bring my sword down on the king's skull, the surrounding air rippled and I was frozen in place.

8

"Eldwin."

Erling's condescending tone filled my ears. He rose from the chair and turned to face me. I still found it odd that such an ugly man had fathered someone as beautiful and kind as Maren. His bald head was oily, and the firelight highlighted it, making his scalp shine. In this light, the red-purplish bruise that ran the length of the left side of his face gave him a sinister appearance.

I strained my muscles, but I couldn't move at all. Erling watched my obvious struggle, and his lips curled in an amused sneer.

"Fight all you want, but you will not get free."

He moved around the chair to stand in front of me and stared into my eyes. I poured all the hatred I had for him into my gaze.

"You are a fool if you thought you could so easily assassinate me. I have eyes everywhere, and nothing gets past my notice. I find it surprising that Anesko sent you to do the deed. Was he too afraid to do it himself? No matter. I'm glad you're here."

Erling lifted his right arm into my view. In his hand, he held a dagger. He placed the tip of the blade against my neck.

"I could slit your throat with hardly an effort," he said.

I'm trapped, I told Sion. *There's some sort of spell keeping me from moving.*

Can you see the one who cast the spell?

I couldn't move my head, but my eyes roamed around the tent. Erling was the only one I could see, but that didn't mean a sorcerer, or several of them, wasn't hidden using magic.

No, I only see the king.

Erling applied pressure to the dagger, causing the tip to break my skin. Warm blood trickled down my neck.

"Lucky for you, I don't want you dead. Not yet, anyway."

He removed the dagger and stepped back, tossing the weapon aside. I wasn't ignorant. He was as sly as a serpent, which meant he wanted something from me. The secret way into the Citadel, most likely. He would be disappointed, then. I would reveal nothing.

Erling made a motion with his hand, an obvious command of some kind, and the spell released my mouth.

"What do you want?" I snarled.

"Many things, as do all men," he replied.

"What do you want from *me*?"

"Ah, now you've asked the right question. I want you to tell me where I can find the Assembly."

"What?"

"Surprised, are you? Did you think I wanted to know how you got out of the Citadel with the barrier still up? I know there are many ways in and out of that blasted place, but I don't care about that. The school will fall when I am ready. What I want first is the Assembly."

If my face wasn't frozen, I would have scowled. "What do you want with the Assembly? They'll never give you an audience with them."

Erling snorted. "I don't need an audience, boy. I'm going to kill them. With their deaths, and the fall of the Order, I will have complete control over Osnen. There will no longer be pockets of power that do not answer to me. This is *my* kingdom."

His words were like a physical blow. He didn't just want to get rid of the Order, he wanted to murder the eldest dragons in the land. Erling was even more wicked than I thought.

"I won't tell you anything."

"I thought you might say that, so I will make myself abundantly clear. If you do not tell me what I want to know, I will destroy everything you care about while I make you watch."

"You can't," I growled. "You'll never get past the barrier."

"*I* don't need to. As I said, I have eyes *everywhere*. Right now, Maren is asleep, yes? And with you out here, there is no one in the school watching over her. Well … no one you'd like to be watching her, anyway."

Erling motioned with his hand and a shadow detached itself from the tent wall. A moment later, the inky blackness faded, revealing a light-haired man in leather armor. He wore a sword strapped at his waist and had the brightest green eyes I had ever seen.

"Show him," Erling said.

The man held his left hand out, palm upward. With his right hand, he traced a circle over his left and flicked his fingers upward. An image appeared between his hands, flickering and distorted, but there was no mistaking what it showed: Maren lying in bed asleep. And standing in the background near the window was a figure holding an unsheathed blade.

"She sleeps heavily tonight," the king murmured.

I swallowed hard. If I hadn't drugged her, she would be able to defend herself.

"Before you think to alert your dragon, know that Maren will be dead before anyone can come to her aid."

"You would kill your own daughter?" I had no doubt that he would, but I hoped there was some small amount of love or mercy in his heart.

"My daughter is already dead. She died to me the day she relinquished her nobility. I have no qualms with killing what remains of her."

"You underestimate her," I said. "When she wakes, she will know she's not alone. Your soldier will be dead before he moves to strike her."

"I am certain she will, which is why you have a limited amount of time to decide on your course of action. If you do not tell me where the Assembly is, I will have him kill her now while you watch."

Do not tell him anything, Sion said. *I will get Master Anesko.*

No! Not yet. Erling isn't lying. Maren will be dead before Anesko can do anything. Do nothing until I tell you to.

If you tell him where the Assembly is, your value is gone and he'll kill you. There is no winning in this situation.

I knew Sion was right, but there had to be another way. The Assembly was searching for Risod, which meant they probably weren't at the Temple of the Bond. Erling would have to navigate the maze, which he wouldn't be able to do without my help. I could lead him around for a while, and by the time we reached it, he would realize the Assembly members weren't there. It would buy me enough time to come up with a plan.

"Tell him to do it," Erling ordered.

"No, wait! I'll tell you!"

Don't fall into his trap, Eldwin!

I know I don't deserve it, but please trust me.

What are you going to do?

I'll figure it out as I go, but do not tell anyone what's happening. Please.

I could feel Sion's hesitation in the bond, but she ultimately agreed.

"I can tell you where their temple is, but you won't be able to find it."

"Why not?" Erling demanded.

"Powerful enchantments protect it. Those who seek the temple with ill will wander the woods around it forever." I didn't know if that last part was true, but it didn't hurt to exaggerate. "You will need someone to lead you through the magical labyrinth."

"Let me guess. That person would be you."

"I've been there before and I know the way. Do not harm Maren and I will take you to the Assembly."

"If you try anything, I'll gut you like a fish," Erling threatened.

"You have my word."

"Your word means nothing to me, lowborn."

I didn't know what else I could offer him, but thankfully, he didn't require any further assurances.

"Take his sword."

The sorcerer did as commanded and removed my blade from my hands, then patted me down for other weapons. He left the war horn, however. Satisfied I was fully disarmed, the sorcerer released his spell. My previous momentum returned, and my hands swung down, slamming painfully against the top of the chair. I hissed in a breath.

"We leave tonight," Erling said to the sorcerer. "Bring the others, as well as anything else you need."

The sorcerer bowed and exited the tent, leaving me alone with Erling. The hate I had for him burned intensely, and I was tempted to attack him with my bare hands, but I knew there were likely other guards hidden in the tent. I would bide my time, and when the opportunity arose, I would strike with fury.

9

WE LEFT WITHIN THE HOUR. I was forced to ride with the sorcerer, whose name I learned was Shadamar. From what I could gather, he was the leader of Erling's private guard. A sorcerer, of all things. Though the more I thought about it, the more it made sense. When there were weapons other than swords and arrows involved, someone skilled with magic would be the best option for protection.

We flew east on the back of a large green dragon whose bulk was so thick that it stretched the straps of the saddle taut and the seams looked as if they might come undone. Erling rode with two others on a blue dragon, one a soldier and the other a sorcerer. Two other dragons, both red, followed behind us, each carrying three guards.

Despite the obvious danger, I enjoyed soaring through the sky in the darkness. The cool evening air ruffled my clothes, and the stars twinkled above. I had a front-row seat to the beauty of the night sky. One thing I didn't like was the further we got from the Citadel, the weaker my bond became. I could still feel Sion's presence, but it was muted, and eventually, we couldn't even speak normally with one another. It was more of an exchange of emotions, much like when we first bonded.

It was a feeling I didn't enjoy.

Regardless, I still had the war horn at my side. If things went badly, I could always use it, though it would take some time for Anesko to reach me, depending on where I was. I resigned myself to star gazing and tried not to think about the man Erling had watching over Maren. It seemed Anesko had not rid our ranks of all the spies, as he believed.

As the time passed, I dozed in the saddle. Shadamar, on the other hand, remained fully alert. It was difficult to determine his age, but he seemed young to me. I wondered how he had gained the attention of the king, but I assumed it was his magical prowess. It was no easy feat to exert control over another person, and he had stopped my attack on the king with ease. I would need to keep an eye on him, as he posed the biggest threat.

I must have fallen asleep, because I jolted suddenly when my stomach lurched. The dragon was descending. I gripped the saddle horn as the dragon continued its descent and wondered briefly if Maren was awake. I prayed she wasn't. She was safer asleep for now. I leaned to the side and scanned the ground, but it was too dark to make out anything other than vague outlines.

"Have we arrived?" I asked loudly.

"Yes," Shadamar answered.

A few moments later, the dragon touched the ground, its immense legs absorbing the impact of its landing. The other dragons landed nearby, the flapping of their wings causing gusts of wind to stir up the area. Ahead, I could see the outlines of trees. How had the time passed so quickly?

"Get down," Shadamar ordered.

I climbed out of the saddle and leaped to the ground, stretching my legs and rubbing my lower back. The king's soldiers also dismounted, and they grouped together. Erling strode over and looked at me.

"Are there any traps we need to worry about?"

I shook my head. "No, none that I'm aware of. The enchantments were affected when magic failed, but there is no danger here."

"Good. Lead the way, then." He glanced at Shadamar. "Stay with him."

I glanced at the sky. It was still dark, but I guessed there were only a couple of hours until dawn. The magical forest would provide its own confusion, but I decided I would lead the king aimlessly around for a while. The Assembly would know we were here, and I hoped they were smart enough to discern what was happening.

"This way," I said.

The woods were eerie in the daylight, and much more so in the dark. Nocturnal animals skittered around in the brush, and the hooting of owls filled the air. There were no obvious trails, not that I would have followed them, anyway. I guided Erling and the others in a circular path, keeping to the outskirts of the forest. None of them caught on, at least for a while.

We were still trudging along when the first rays of sunlight peeked over the horizon, painting the sky with a palette of vibrant reds, oranges, and pinks. The colors of the forest became visible as daylight spilled across the land, and the chirping of birds replaced the nighttime sounds. I frowned. Something wasn't right. The forest had always been quiet, unnervingly so, yet it sounded full of life.

"What is taking so long?" Erling demanded. "I'm certain we've come this way already. What are you up to?"

"Nothing," I replied. "As I said, this place has powerful enchantments on it. The Temple of the Bond isn't found, it finds you."

"That makes no sense. What do you feel, Shadamar?"

The sorcerer gazed around the forest. "He is telling the truth. Ancient magic permeates this place, but it is … distorted. I cannot tell one enchantment from another. I'm afraid we are at his mercy."

Erling glared at me. "No more games. Take us to the temple or Maren dies."

There was no way for him to know whether I was fooling with him, but I didn't want to press my luck. Maren was too important to me.

"Empty whatever is in your minds. The magic will not allow us entrance if it knows your intentions are ill."

Shadamar looked at the king. "Do as he says."

I waited a moment, then continued through the woods, subtly angling our direction toward the center of the forest. I knew we were on the right course when I began to see things that weren't there. From my periphery, I could see shadows among the trees whispering and pointing at us, but when I looked at them directly, they were gone.

Yes, I told myself. *This is the way.*

The exhaustion and drowsiness set in slowly, and I could see the concern growing on Shadamar's face.

"Don't worry," I said, my words slurring slightly. "This is normal. It's the work of ... the work of ... of the magic."

Erling was the first to collapse. Shadamar stopped but made no move to assist him. Neither did any of the others. They were all fighting the effects of the magic, but one by one, they all dropped to the forest floor. Shadamar was the last of Erling's men to do so. The last thing that rolled around in my mind before I fell face-first onto the leafy ground was surprise, surprise that I stayed conscious longer than the sorcerer.

10

When I opened my eyes, I was staring at Shadamar's boots.

I pushed myself up onto my hands and knees and looked straight. The black stones of the Temple of the Bond glinted under the sun. Nemryth was standing a few feet away, a scowl plastered on her face.

"Why did you lead them here?" she demanded.

"I'm sorry. I had no choice. You must leave. Now. The king seeks your destruction."

"We will not leave our home. If the king wants a fight, I will give him one."

"No." I shook my head. "He has a soldier watching Maren. If you kill the king, the soldier will kill her."

Nemryth stared at me for a long moment in silence.

"Fine," she said. "We're still searching for Risod, so that will give us an excuse to leave the temple. How long do you need?"

An idea came to me.

"Is there anything of Risod's you can give me?"

"Why?"

"The king wants to find you, but because of the enchantments of the forest, he wasn't able to. He needed me to show him. I'm sure his sorcerer here," I kicked Shadamar's foot, "can track Risod down if he had one of her belongings. It's how someone found me once. He will lead us to the dragon slayers, and if all goes well, they'll wipe each other out."

Nemryth smirked, and I knew she liked my plan.

"That's clever of you," she said. "I will leave something out for them to find. Once they are on the trail, we will follow you."

"Don't let them see you or that will throw off everything."

"They will not detect our presence."

I nodded. "You should go before they wake up."

Nemryth chuckled. "You know we control when the magic lets you wake up, don't you? They will not come to until I let them. It is the only thing about the enchantments that has not changed."

I did not know that, but it was great news.

"Put me back to sleep," I said. "And let the king wake before me. This needs to be believable."

"As you wish. We will leave now. It won't take long. Hopefully, this works."

"It will," I said. It had to.

"See you soon."

The grogginess washed over me, and I crumpled to the ground. The next thing I knew, someone was shaking my shoulder. I opened my eyes to see Erling standing over me. His guards were gathered around him, weapons drawn.

"Get up," Erling said.

I wasn't sure how long I had been down, but the sun wasn't much further into the sky. Rising to my feet, I glanced around the clearing.

"Where are they?"

I pointed at the temple. "They should be inside there."

"Take the lead," he ordered.

I walked across the clearing and ascended the steps. The king and his men followed at a distance. He was being wary. I pushed against the doors, but they didn't budge.

"It's locked," I said, looking over my shoulder.

Erling nodded his head at Shadamar. "Open them."

The sorcerer joined me near the doors and held his right hand up. He flicked his gaze at me. "Get behind me."

I did as he said. A bright light flashed into existence, temporarily blinding me. A moment later, the sound of splintering wood filled the air. When my vision came back, I saw Shadamar's spell had blasted the doors to pieces. He strode into the temple, a flickering red-orange ball of flame in his hand. Erling and the rest of his men streamed into the building, one of them pulling me forcefully along.

"Split up," the king said. "Search everywhere."

"You're with me," Shadamar said, motioning for me to follow him.

I figured if I did everything without question, it might be suspicious. I folded my arms across my chest.

"I'll stay here. This is your suicide mission, not mine."

One of the soldiers behind me kicked me in the back of my right knee, dropping me to the floor. I gritted my teeth against the pain and anger.

"The next order you ignore will cost you a limb," the man threatened.

I slowly climbed back to my feet and shot him a glare. The soldier was grinning like an idiot, clearly amused.

"Do as Shadamar says," Erling said. "He holds the power over Maren's life."

That reminder helped keep my focus on the plan. I followed Shadamar as he traversed the halls on the western side of the temple. We entered room after room, all of them empty. There were no beds or anything else, just cold rooms of stone.

"Maybe they knew you were coming," I said.

Shadamar whirled around, the ball of flame crackling inches from my face. "Did you warn them?"

"How would I? I'm not bonded to any of them."

The sorcerer gave me an intense stare before turning around and continuing his search. The last door at the end of the hall had a silver plaque with a red gem in it. It was a ruby. I assumed it was Risod's personal chambers. Shadamar pushed the door open, and we stepped inside. It was the first room that showed any signs of someone's presence. There was a neatly made bed, a side table with a lantern, and at the end of the bed was a large storage chest.

"Open the chest," Shadamar said.

I begrudgingly obeyed. There were some clothes at the bottom, but what caught my eye was an ornate dagger in a leather sheath. The pommel of the blade held a ruby that seemed to glow with a light of its own. I grabbed it and held it up.

"I found this."

"Hand it over."

I gave it to the sorcerer and glanced around the room as he studied the weapon. There was nothing else of interest.

"Can you use that to track them or something?" I asked, trying to sound helpful.

Shadamar stuffed the dagger into his belt and left the room. I hurried after him and we returned to the main chamber. The others were already there.

"There's no one here," Erling said. "If you led me on a wild goose chase, I'll—"

"This is the right place," Shadamar interrupted. "They may not be here now, but I can find them."

"How?"

"With this." Shadamar held up the dagger. "It has a magical connection to something else, something one of them has on their person. I can use it to find them."

I found it funny that the sorcerer took credit for my idea, but it didn't matter. As long as the king bought into it, that was all that mattered.

"Any idea where they would be?" Erling asked, looking at me.

"No. As far as I'm aware, they never leave this place."

Erling looked at Shadamar and nodded. The sorcerer closed his eyes and muttered words under his breath. The silence stretched on, and I worried the dagger might not have been the item Nemryth intended us to find. When Shadamar opened his eyes, a red glow emanated from his pupils.

"I can see the trail," he said. "We must go west."

Erling smiled, likely thinking he was on the verge of victory.

"Move out," he commanded. "Let's find these blasted dragons."

11

WE FLEW WEST FOR SEVERAL hours, Shadamar's spell guiding us. Little did he know, he was leading the king to his doom. I tried not to glance back too often, but the times I did, I saw no sign of the Assembly members. Either we had lost them, or they were doing an amazing job of hiding.

It was risky for me to be there when the king's men encountered the dragon slayers, but I figured it would give me the opportunity to slip away and escape. Given how my plans usually worked out, that likely wouldn't happen, but I could hope.

My thoughts strayed to what the dragon slayers were doing in Osnen. Nemryth thought they arrived on accident, and at first, I did, too … but now I wasn't so sure. Hunting dragons was what they did, but the fact they captured a member of the Assembly didn't seem to be a coincidence.

Morning turned to noon, and my stomach growled. I hadn't eaten since dinner the night before, and hunger was clawing at me. The king and his men had breakfast, but of course, they didn't share their food with me. With a minor amount of luck, I'd find something to eat after escaping.

The sun was in the middle of the sky, but the breeze that whipped around me as we flew made the heat unnoticeable. The landscape below gradually changed, and soon, I could see the city of Tiradale in the distance. Now I knew exactly where I was. The dragon we rode veered left of the city, heading in a southern direction.

"We're close," Shadamar shouted. "It isn't much farther."

I instinctively reached for my sword and then remembered the sorcerer had taken it from me. It was my father's blade, and I couldn't leave it behind. I didn't know where it was, either, and I cursed the man under my breath.

A thin line of smoke drifted into the sky, and I spotted the camp. It was nestled among a few small hills. Several tents were encircled around a cooking fire, but I didn't see any movement. The dragon began a slow circling descent and landed a fair distance from the camp. Erling's mount landed next, followed by the others. I climbed down and traced my fingers along the smooth wood of the war horn at my waist. I'd almost forgotten I had it.

"Why did we land here?" Erling asked as he strode to where Shadamar and I stood.

"He refuses to get closer," the sorcerer replied, motioning to the dragon. "He smells something he doesn't like."

Did the dragon slayers have some sort of deterrent? Or maybe the dragon could sense their enchanted weapons, designed specifically to kill his kind.

"Stubborn creatures. We go on foot, then. The dragons can provide support from the sky."

Shadamar was silent for a moment. "He refuses to get any closer."

Erling's face hardened, but there was little he could do. It was impossible to force a dragon's will.

"I didn't see anyone in the camp," Erling said, changing the subject. "They must be in the tents."

Shadamar nodded. "That was my thought as well. They don't know we're coming, so we have the advantage."

"There are five of them and ten of us. The numbers are doubled in our favor."

Shadamar frowned. "There are nine of us, my Lord. You should stay back with the prisoner to ensure your safety. We don't know what they are capable of, or if more have joined them."

"We are all going, including Eldwin." Erling drew his sword.

"As you say." Shadamar also unsheathed his blade, and I saw it was my sword.

"That's mine," I said.

"Not anymore." Shadamar smirked at me, and I wanted nothing more than to punch him in the face.

Without another word, Erling turned and marched toward the hills that surrounded the camp. Shadamar nodded for me to follow, and I trudged after the king. The rest of the soldiers walked behind us. The hills weren't too steep, and we swiftly crested them.

Below, I counted five tents. The material they were made of looked like leather, but there was something strange about the patterns on them. Each one was unique, but there was nothing uniform about any of them. They were irregular and looked like …

My eyes widened. They made their tents of dragon hide. Revulsion overwhelmed me and I felt bile rise in my throat. I quickly swallowed to keep it down and looked at Erling. Either he didn't notice, or he didn't care. I was certain it was the latter.

"Two to a tent," Erling said. "Keep a close eye on Eldwin here. We don't need him running off."

Shadamar pressed the tip of his sword—*my sword*—into my back and prodded me painfully with it. I hesitantly scaled down the hill and reached the bottom without too much trouble. I was concerned that if Shadamar slipped and tumbled down, he'd accidentally impale me, but thankfully, he kept his balance.

Erling took a step forward, and Shadamar grabbed him by the arm, pulling him back. Erling's scowl caused the sorcerer to falter, but he cleared his throat.

"Forgive me, but we should send someone else ahead first."

"Is there a trap?"

"I don't sense anything, but not all traps are made of magic."

Erling grunted in reply and nodded his agreement. Shadamar looked at the other sorcerer, the one who rode with the king, and he pointed. He held a finger up to his lips, indicating he should be quiet. The man bowed his head and walked ahead stealthily. I watched him draw nearer to the camp and wondered why the dragon slayers hadn't made an appearance yet. Were they asleep in the middle of the day?

They couldn't all be, not if they held Risod captive. The man angled right, heading for the tent closest to him. His steps grew more confident the closer he got, and the other soldiers shuffled forward eagerly. The hairs on my arms stood on end, and as quickly as I blinked, the sorcerer crossed some sort of invisible line that set off a ward. An explosion shook the ground. I crouched down and shielded my face with my right arm.

Dust and debris showered the area, and the power of the blast tore a trench in the earth. The sorcerer's mutilated body lay in a heap twenty feet away from where he'd been. Everything was silent for a long moment. Erling and the others were clearly surprised, and before any of them could recover their wits, the dragon slayers rushed out from their tents.

Erling was the first to move. He rushed forward, clashing swords with a tall brute covered in tattooed markings. The other soldiers followed their king's example and engaged the enemy. I stumbled backward and looked up the hill. It was the perfect opportunity to escape, but that meant leaving my father's sword behind. It also meant risking Maren's life in the event the king and his men overpowered the slayers.

The battle was raging fiercely, and both sides seemed evenly matched. The clanging of swords reverberated through the air, and for a moment, I thought the king would be victorious. One of his soldiers fell, cut down by a man wielding an axe. I recognized him from my previous encounter with the slayers. He roared in triumph and cut down another soldier. Another slayer, a woman in chain mail, struck a mortal wound to the soldier beside Shadamar.

Half of Erling's men had fallen, and not a single slayer was dead or injured. I stared at Shadamar, cursing the man again for taking my father's sword. I chewed on my lower lip and decided to cut my losses. There was no way Erling was going to win this battle now. I started to climb the hill and looked back when I heard a scream of pain. The tattooed brute had driven his sword into Erling's leg.

Good, I thought. *Let him suffer and die.*

A thunderclap roared, the sound so loud I involuntarily cowered and lost my footing. I fell and rolled back down the hill. A blazing white light surrounded Shadamar, and it expanded outward, turning several dragon slayers into ash. I spotted Risod as she was dragged from one of the tents by a slayer who had not been part of the battle. The remaining slayers fled, and Shadamar dropped to his knees.

12

I SCRAMBLED ONTO MY FEET and ran to where Shadamar was, intending to take my sword from him. As I reached for it, I froze in place, just as I had in the king's tent. Apparently, Shadamar was not as exhausted as he appeared. He glared at me and rose to his feet, then strode past to where Erling was crying out in agony, leaving me unable to move.

After a long moment of screaming, Erling fell silent, and I wondered if he was dead. Shadamar released me from the spell and I turned to look. Erling was still lying on the ground, but Shadamar had tied off his leg to slow the bleeding.

"Help me carry him," the sorcerer said. "We need to get him to a healer."

I scoffed at the request. "I'd rather let him lie there and bleed to death."

Shadamar pointed the sword at me. "You will help me or Maren will die, and then I'll kill you."

Sion had offered to get help, and I'd told her not to. I regretted that now. While the distance wasn't as great between us, I still couldn't communicate with her. Her emotions came through the bond clearly, mostly curiosity, but I couldn't use emotions to instruct her what to do. Until we closed the distance further, I would have to continue to play the obedient prisoner.

With an exaggerated sigh, I walked over and knelt beside Erling. The wound in his leg was a gaping hole about two inches in diameter. Blood soaked his pants and stained the ground beneath him. I was no expert, but I didn't think he would survive long enough to reach a healer.

"We need to pull him up by his arms," Shadamar said. "I've done the best I could with his leg, but we'll need to be careful."

I glanced up the hill. Although it wasn't too steep, dragging a limp body up it would hardly be a simple task. Erling was lucky his sorcerer hadn't died like the rest of his men. There was something fitting about letting him bleed out all alone, but alas, we didn't always get what we wanted.

"Can't you just use your magic to fly him up there?" I asked.

"If I could, do you think I'd be asking for help to carry him? He is protected against magic."

A lot made sense with that information, though I wondered how that worked. Did he have some sort of talisman that negated magic near him, or was it something else?

"Quit gawking and help me," Shadamar demanded.

We each grabbed one of his arms and pulled him up. It was a challenge because he was deadweight, but also because Shadamar was trying to keep the king's injured leg from moving too much. Once we had his arms slung across our shoulders, we started the trek up the hill. The going was slow and precarious, but we eventually reached the top and Shadamar cursed.

The dragons were gone.

I scanned the sky, but there was no sign of them. They must have fled when the battle erupted. That, or the smell of the dragon hide tents was enough to keep them from sticking around. I didn't blame them for leaving, but it was a major inconvenience. We stood there for a long moment, and I assumed Shadamar was trying to decide what to do.

"I'm surprised your dragon abandoned you," I said, side-eyeing him.

"I am not bonded to a dragon," he replied.

"Why not?"

"It is a weakness I do not need."

He couldn't have been more wrong. Being bonded to a dragon was not a weakness, but a strength.

"You know as well as I do he will not make it, even if the dragons were still here."

"You better hope not. If the king dies, so does Maren."

"Why do you serve him?" I asked, growing aggravated. "He's a tyrant."

"Do not concern yourself with that," Shadamar said. "We have to get him to Tiradale."

"How do you expect to do that? We have no way to transport him."

"I will make a stretcher."

"And do what? Carry him the entire way? Tiradale is miles from here."

"Yes," Shadamar said. "We will carry him. Here, set him down."

We laid Erling down on the ground. He groaned softly, but remained unconscious.

"Stay here. If you try to run, you won't get far."

Shadamar went back down the hill to the camp. I turned my gaze east and searched the sky for the Assembly, but I still didn't see them. Where were they? Why hadn't they arrived yet? Since there was nothing else to do but wait, I sat on the ground beside the king. His breathing was shallow and his skin was pale.

I looked down at the camp and watched Shadamar as he worked. He cut a portion of dragon hide from one of the tents, then chopped one of the tent poles in half and attached the hide to the pieces. His hands glowed as he ran them along the poles, fusing the material to the wooden shafts. When he finished, he had a makeshift litter. Shadamar carried it up the hill and set it down next to Erling.

"Grab his legs and lift as gently as you can."

I reluctantly did so, scrunching my face in disgust when my hand touched warm blood. Shadamar was going above and beyond what I would expect for a man who was certainly dying. Why was he so loyal to Erling? What had the king promised him? I didn't bother to ask, since I knew the man would tell me nothing.

We set Erling on the litter and I knelt and brushed my hand against the ground, trying to remove the blood. My head snapped to look at Erling as a loud gasp escaped him. His eyes fluttered open.

"Easy, my Lord," Shadamar said. "Don't move. You are injured, but I will get you somewhere safe."

I doubted the king was coherent enough to understand him, but he turned his head to the side to look at the sorcerer.

"Assembly?" he wheezed.

Shadamar shook his head, casting a baleful look in my direction. "They were not here. We need to leave before the slayers return."

"I'm not going anywhere with you," I said. "Not unless you guarantee Maren's safety and call off your war against the Order."

"You have nothing to bargain with!" Shadamar snapped.

"Without my help, the king will bleed to death. It seems we are at an impasse."

"I will do it," Erling said weakly.

"My Lord?"

"If he will help, I will do as … as he asks." Erling's face tensed with pain and he fell back into unconsciousness, his head lolling to the side awkwardly.

I was no fool. The king was lying to get what he wanted. A small part of me hoped he would realize his folly, but that depended on him surviving, which didn't seem likely to me.

"Are you satisfied?" Shadamar asked.

Of course, I wasn't, but the alternative was too risky. Once we reached Tiradale, I'd be close enough to communicate with Sion. She could inform Anesko about what was happening, and I was confident he could deal with the soldier watching over Maren. With her safety guaranteed, I would be free to finish off the king. The only thing that stood in my way was Shadamar.

I needed to get rid of him.

13

I FOUND SOME FOOD IN the camp and devoured it, partially because I was ravenously hungry and partially because Shadamar rushed me at sword point. With a full stomach, I felt more energized. Shadamar forced me to walk at the front of the litter, which I assumed was because he wanted to keep his eyes on me.

We walked for hours before Shadamar allowed for a brief break beside a slow-moving stream. I drank my fill and soaked my hands in the cool water, easing the discomfort. Several blisters had formed on my palms from the friction of holding the tent poles for so long, and my arm muscles throbbed with soreness.

"Let's get back to it," Shadamar said.

I sighed and rose to my feet, waving my hands back and forth to fling the water from them. Erling remained unconscious, but his bleeding had stopped. His chest moved up and down with his feeble breath. I thought about telling the sorcerer that we were toiling in vain, but I was too tired to argue with him.

We picked up the litter and continued until dusk descended over the land and the city of Tiradale came into view. It surprised me at how quickly we covered the distance and assumed I must have overjudged how far from the city we had been.

At the gates, Shadamar informed the city guards of what had transpired and one of them rushed off to notify the baron. It seemed like ages since I had last been in Tiradale, but the city had changed little. The streets bustled with activity, and upbeat music from a nearby tavern drifted into the air.

It wasn't long before more guards arrived. They took over carrying the litter, for which I was thankful, but then they escorted us through the city to the castle. When Maren and I had come here to investigate the missing children, we'd entered the castle grounds through the side gate. The crowds parted to make way for us, and the soldiers led us straight through the main entrance.

Baron Giffor and a retinue of servants were waiting in the courtyard. Healers in white robes immediately inundated the soldiers carrying the litter. I watched wordlessly, surprised that the baron's loyalty didn't waver with the king in such a vulnerable state.

"My lord," Shadamar greeted, offering a tired bow. "I apologize for intruding on you, but your city was the closest that could help."

Giffor waved his words away. "Nonsense. It's the least I can do for the king."

Realization struck me suddenly that the baron might be thinking of how he could benefit from helping Erling. Perhaps there was more reward for him in doing that than trying to usurp the throne. Court politics were far from my realm of knowledge. With everyone's attention on the king, it would be easier to slip away unnoticed.

"Take him to the infirmary," Giffor ordered.

The soldiers holding the litter marched off, and Shadamar started to go with them.

"He's in excellent hands," the baron said.

"I do not doubt the talents of your people, my lord. It is my duty to keep watch over the king at all times."

"A man of loyalty. I respect that. If it makes you feel more at ease, we can walk with them."

"Please," Shadamar said.

Now is my chance, I thought.

"This one is a prisoner of the king," the sorcerer added, looking at me.

Giffor turned his attention in my direction, and his eyes widened in shock. "El … Elfin?"

"Eldwin," I corrected.

"Ah, yes. You managed to get into trouble with the king, did you? Not a wise move."

"The king is a tyrant," I spat. "And his accusations are baseless."

The baron exchanged looks with Shadamar.

"He stays with me," the sorcerer said.

"Very well." He motioned to one of his guards and the man came to stand beside me. "Keep an eye on him."

We followed the litter into the castle and I listened to the two of them talk.

"As soon as your healers have done their work, we need to get the king back to the Citadel. Are there any riders here that can take us?"

"I'm afraid not," Giffor said. "They were all withdrawn to the Citadel, per the king's request. He can stay here as long as necessary."

"You are too kind, but there are matters that still need to be dealt with that require his presence there."

Shadamar glanced back at me and leaned in close to the baron, lowering his voice so that I couldn't make out what he said. I didn't have to hear his words to know what it was about. The king was a snake, and he would never keep his word about ending his war. I reached out through the bond.

Sion? Can you hear me?

I can. Where are you?

Her presence within my mind was a wave of comfort, and I relished the feeling.

I'm in Tiradale. The king was attacked by the dragon slayers, and I'm being held prisoner.

I am coming to you. I will raze the city if they harm you.

No, stay at the Citadel. I need you to deliver a message to Anesko.

What is it?

There is a soldier there that the king employs. He's watching Maren and plans to kill her if I don't do whatever the king wants. Anesko needs to find him.

I will tell him, Sion said. *And then I am coming to get you.*

Do not risk your safety for mine. Anesko will not lower the barrier for you unless it is a matter of life or death. I am safe for now. If that changes, I will tell you.

Sion rumbled through the bond, her aggravation evident.

Besides, I'm waiting for an opportunity to kill the king. He's tougher than I thought, and now that he's with Baron Giffor's healers, he's probably going to pull through his injury. I just have to figure out how to get his sorcerer to leave his side.

Kill him, too.

Were it so easy, I'd have already done so. He's as powerful as Maren, if not more so.

I will ask Anesko if there is anyone in Tiradale loyal to the Order, she said. *Perhaps we have allies there who can help.*

I doubt it, but it doesn't hurt to ask.

We turned down a wide hall, and they carried the king into a chamber that looked similar to the infirmary at the Citadel. The soldiers set the litter down on the floor and stepped aside, allowing the healers to take over. They gently lifted him onto a cot and continued their work. Giffor dismissed all the soldiers except the one keeping watch over me and turned his attention back to Shadamar.

"I can give you horses," he said. "They are fast, but I don't foresee the king being able to ride any time soon."

Shadamar's brow creased. "We will see how he is doing in the morning. He may surprise us."

"He may indeed." Giffor flicked his gaze to me. "What of him?"

"Lock him in the dungeon."

14

My cell didn't feel like it was in the dungeon. It was clean and well-lit. There were a few other prisoners, but they were on the farther end of the corridor. A small cot was in the corner, but considering they chained me to the wall, I couldn't reach it, so I sat on the floor with my back pressed against the cold stone wall.

The guard on duty gave me a hunk of bread. It wasn't much, nor was it fresh, but it filled my stomach and sated my hunger. Eventually, the guard walked down the corridor, extinguishing the lanterns. Left in the dark with only my thoughts, and utterly exhausted, I leaned my head back and stared at the shadows above me.

It was impossible to judge the passage of time, and I closed my eyes to rest them for a moment. The clank of the cell door woke me, and I squinted against the glow of a lantern. Was it morning already? My eyes slowly adjusted, and I sat up. The chill in the cell had grown, and I rubbed my arms.

"What is it?" I asked.

"Eldwin. Are you hurt?"

I knew that voice. I stared at the figure holding the lantern until the details of her face became clear.

"Master Katori? What are you doing here?"

"I've come to rescue you."

She placed the lantern on a hook on the wall, then knelt and unlocked my shackles with an iron key attached to a thick ring. I flexed my wrists and stood up.

"Is Maren safe?"

"Yes," Katori replied. "Anesko got the message you gave Sion. We have dealt with the spy."

"Dealt with?"

"He was executed."

Relief washed over me. "That's great."

"Death is never something to be applauded," she said.

"No, that's not what I meant. I'm just glad she's out of harm's way. Are you the only one here?"

"Yes. Anesko did not want to risk lowering the barrier to let Sion out, so I left the same way you did."

I nodded. Now that Maren was safe, I could leave and there was nothing Shadamar or Erling could do about it. Erling.

"I know where the king is," I said.

"What do you mean?"

"I left the Citadel to kill him. Things didn't go as planned, and the dragon slayers injured him. He's in the infirmary."

"I'm sure the baron has guards watching over him."

"Maybe, but I'm not worried about them. It's Shadamar I'm worried about."

"Who is Shadamar?"

"The king's personal guard. He's a sorcerer, so I will need your help."

"Anesko told me to get you out of here and return to the Citadel. We should go before someone sees us."

I shook my head. "I can't go back, not until the king is dead. We have the chance to end this war here and now. I can't do it without you."

Katori heaved a resigned sigh. "Very well. Lead the way."

I smiled and hurried out of the cell. The way here had been easy to memorize, and I backtracked the way the guards had brought me. We didn't encounter any soldiers along the way, but we kept to the shadows when possible and slipped through the castle halls as quietly as we could. Once we reached the chamber that led to the infirmary hall, I paused.

Two guards were standing at the entrance to the hall. They were talking, clearly not expecting any trouble. While they wore swords strapped at their waists, they weren't wearing proper armor.

"We need to get rid of them," I whispered.

"I'll put them to sleep."

"No. If you use magic, Shadamar might sense it."

"What do you propose, then?"

I looked around the chamber, and my gaze landed on a metal sconce on the wall.

"I have an idea. Follow me."

Taking the sconce off the wall, I carried it out in front of me and approached the guards. They stopped talking and moved to block the way ahead.

"This way is off limits," one of them said.

"Apologies, sir. A prisoner escaped, and the captain sent us to ensure he didn't go after the king."

The guards exchanged looks, which was the opening I needed. I swung the sconce into the side of one guard's head. A sickening crack echoed off the walls, and the man collapsed on the floor. The other guard stumbled backward into the hall, drawing his sword. I rushed forward, waving the sconce back and forth wildly.

The soldier brought his blade up and it clanged against the sconce. The sound reverberating along the hall. I cursed, hoping it didn't alert Shadamar or any other guards. Katori pushed past me and drove her fist into the guard's side. He grunted and tried to back up further, but we closed in on him. I jabbed the pointed end of the sconce at him while Katori dropped low and swept his legs out from under him. He landed on his rear end and Katori followed through with a knee to his head, knocking him unconscious.

"We need to hurry," she huffed. "The noise will surely have caught someone's attention."

"This way."

I led her to the infirmary and peered around the doorway. Erling was still lying in the same bed, and Shadamar was sleeping in chair beside him. No other guards were present. That seemed foolish to me, but then again, there was no reason to believe the king would be in danger within the baron's walls.

"There," I whispered, pointing. "That's the sorcerer."

"I will deal with him."

I entered the room and saw my sword lying on the floor at Shadamar's feet, within easy range if he needed it. Stepping quietly, I retrieved it and stared at the sorcerer, wondering again why he was so loyal to Erling. I nodded at Katori and unsheathed the blade, gently poking Shadamar in the chest with it. His eyes cracked open, and it took him a moment to realize what was happening. He moved to rise from the chair, but before he could, Katori finished uttering the words to a spell that froze him in place, much like he had done to me in Erling's pavilion.

"Sleeping on the job? That's a shame. Do you remember how you threatened to kill my wife? To kill me?"

I pressed the tip of my sword against Erling's ribcage. Shadamar's eyes filled with rage, but he could do nothing.

"Erling's reign of tyranny is over. I want you to see him die so that you suffer, knowing that you were powerless to save him. You don't like the feeling, do you? I imagine not. Now you know how it feels."

I held Shadamar's gaze and steeled myself for what needed to be done. For all my talk, it was no easy task to take another person's life. I reminded myself of the terrible things Erling had said to me, the way he treated the people of the kingdom that he viewed as beneath him. All of it helped fuel my anger, and with one swift move, I forced my sword through Erling's side and into his heart.

He made a noise in his throat. I stood still, hardly believing I actually did it. The king was dead by my hand. I twisted the hilt, opening the wound further, then jerked my blade free. Blood poured from the wound, staining the bed and running off onto the floor. I looked at Katori.

"It is done," she hissed. "Let us go."

I wiped the blood off my sword using Erling's body, then sheathed the weapon and strapped it to the belt around my waist. Shadamar's eyes were watery with tears, but the rage in his gaze only intensified.

"Never forget this act," I told him.

Katori and I left the room, and a part of me died with the king.

15

WE RETURNED TO THE CITADEL on the winds of magic, thanks to Katori. She transported us to the hidden door outside the walls. It was still dark, but I assumed dawn would arrive soon.

"Tell Sion we've returned."

I reached through the bond and touched Sion's mind. She was sleeping, but sensing my presence, she quickly awoke.

Katori and I are here, I said.

The bond flooded with her enthusiasm. It was infectious, and I couldn't stop smiling despite my feelings toward what I'd done. That, and although I'd only been away a few days, not being able to speak with her had been more miserable than I realized.

I will inform Master Anesko.

We waited in silence, not even daring to risk whispering to one another for fear someone would hear us. I kept my eyes to the south and watched the flicking firelights of the enemy encampment. After a few moments, which felt longer because of my impatience, the hidden door in the wall slid open. I knelt and looked through. Anesko was there, along with Curate Henrik and Maren.

"You first," I said, looking up at Katori.

She dropped onto her hand and knees and crawled through. The barrier returned, sizzling the disrupted dirt. I watched Anesko and waited. As soon as the barrier came down again, I hurried across the threshold.

"Eldwin!"

Maren embraced me before I was fully back on my feet, and we tumbled to the ground. She kissed me fiercely, and I returned it with equal passion.

"I'm sorry," I whispered, flicking my gaze at the others. "I shouldn't have—"

"I'm not mad at you, Eldwin. I mean, I was at first, but I'm just glad you're all right."

Anesko stepped close and cleared his throat. "I hate to intrude on your private moment, but I must know. Were you successful?"

I looked from Maren to Anesko and back.

"Yes. The king is dead."

Maren gave a slight nod, her expression giving no hint of her emotions. Her eyes, however, told another story. It was like looking into a mirror and seeing my inner turmoil on display.

"Then it is over," Anesko said. It could have been my imagination, but it seemed as though an invisible weight lifted from him, and his shoulders rose.

"It was in the baron's castle in Tiradale," I added. "Only one of his sorcerers knows. He was the only one who survived with us."

"The news won't reach his camp until morning, I'm sure. You've done us a great service, Eldwin."

I knew his words were true, but they rang hollow. "I only did what any of us would have done."

"You strode into great danger at the behest of others. Few would willingly do so. Sunrise will be upon us soon. Let us try to get some rest. Who knows what awaits us when the news arrives."

Maren climbed off me and helped me to my feet. I brushed my backside off and the five of us walked together through the courtyard. Aside from a few guards on the walls, there was no one else out at this hour. Our footsteps were the only noise. They sounded so loud echoing off the stone walls.

We entered the school and before everyone parted ways, Anesko said, "Come see me in the morning. I want to know everything."

"We can meet now if you'd prefer. There's something I need to speak with you about, anyway."

"Surely it can wait until the morning? I am weary to the bone."

We needed to take a group of riders out to find the Assembly and deal with the dragon slayers, but I knew that until the army camped outside the walls was gone, Anesko would not consider lowering the barrier.

"It can wait," I said.

He offered a tired smile in thanks and strode off down the hall. Maren wrapped her right arm around my left and we headed for our room.

"I'm sorry," I told her again.

"It's fine."

"No, it isn't. I …" Would her anger reignite if she knew why she had fallen asleep that night? "I forced you to stay here."

"You did? I don't remember that."

"That's because I slipped something into your drink that caused you to fall asleep."

Maren went silent, and I was certain she was about to give me a verbal lashing.

"I see."

An awkward silence stretched between us until we reached the door to our shared chamber.

"I understand if you hate me now," I whispered.

"Oh, Eldwin. I could never hate you. You are not perfect, but neither am I. I tried to make a decision that would affect both our lives without even stopping to consider your thoughts."

She turned to face me, and I saw her eyes were wet with tears. A host of emotions rose within me, and though I tried desperately to hold them back, they poured forth as tears. I buried my head into her shoulder and sobbed. She clung tightly to me, and we shared a moment unlike any we'd experienced before.

I don't know how long we stood like that, but eventually, we released one another and wordlessly entered our room. I pulled my boots off and removed my dirty clothes, climbing into bed with only my undergarments on. Maren scooted close to me, and I fell asleep almost instantly.

The clanging of a bell startled me, and I looked at the window. Light streamed through the stained glass, bathing the floor in a spectrum of colors.

"What is that?" Maren asked, sitting up.

"It's the bell, but it shouldn't be going off now."

We exchanged looks, and as if reading each other's minds, we leaped out of bed and got dressed, hurrying through the halls. We passed Surrel, and I looked over at her questioningly.

"Any idea what's going on?"

"I'm afraid not."

I nodded, and we picked up the pace, joining a small group who were heading for the front entrance of the school. No one seemed to know what the bell was for, and as we stepped into the courtyard, I spotted Anesko. Even he seemed confused. A guard from the walls rushed down the rampart steps and skidded to a halt in front of him.

"Is the enemy leaving?" Anesko asked.

"No, sir. Heralds are approaching under a white banner," the guard huffed.

Maren and I joined them, and Curate Henrik wasn't far behind us.

"Perhaps they've come to announce their withdraw," Henrik suggested.

"Yes, perhaps," Anesko sagely nodded. "I am surprised the encampment is not overcome with chaos by now. If the generals have learned of the king's death, they should be fighting for power."

"All seems calm so far," the guard replied.

"Let us see what they want, then."

We hurried to the ramparts and watched as the heralds approached. The distance made it difficult to see their faces, but I counted at least a dozen men.

"Why so many to announce a withdraw?" I asked.

No one answered, but I didn't expect anyone to. Once the group was just outside the range of our archers, they stopped and waved their banners back and forth.

"I will go out and speak with them," Anesko announced.

"What if it's a trap?" Henrik asked.

"Not even the late king would dare violate the white flag."

While I doubted that was true, it didn't feel right for Anesko to go out there alone. I laid a hand on his shoulder.

"I'm coming with you."

"As am I," Maren said.

"Then we shall go as well." Katori motioned to herself and Henrik.

"You two stay here," Anesko replied, looking at them. "Eldwin and Maren will be plenty."

The three of us returned to the courtyard and waited for the men in the guardhouse to open the southern gates. If it was a trap, at least the enemy would have some trouble with us before they reached Autumnwick.

Three horses were brought for us, and we waited for the barrier to be removed. The portion covering the gates flickered and faded, and we rode out to meet the heralds. As we drew closer, I noticed that one of them was wearing a dark cape, his face concealed by its hood.

"Hail," Anesko greeted, stopping his mount a dozen paces from the heralds.

"His Majesty wishes to speak with you," one of them said. The front riders made a path for the hooded man, and he flicked the reins in his hand, urging his horse forward slowly.

"I heard the king was dead." Anesko's demeanor suddenly became wary.

The figure pulled his hood back, and my eyes widened in surprise. It was Shadamar.

"Erling is dead, and now I rule over Osnen."

Shadmar turned his gaze to me. "You didn't just kill a king," he said. "You killed a brother."

Many things suddenly made sense, especially the reason for his steadfast devotion to Erling. He turned his attention to Maren.

"Niece."

"Uncle."

My heart was pounding in my chest. Shadamar was Erling's brother. How had I not seen it before? The two bore little resemblance, but still. It was so obvious now that I knew. And I had made him watch as I killed his brother.

"I have come to tell you that I am withdrawing my forces. The kingdom will grieve the loss of her former king, and celebrate the rise of her new one. Savor your victory, for it is a fleeting one. I will return to wipe the Order from the face of Osnen, and not even the history books will mention you."

Shadamar looked at me again. "You told me not to forget what you did. I won't."

He turned his mount around and spurred the beast back toward the camp.

16

It took the better part of a week, but eventually, the king's forces left the area, leaving an enormous swath of flattened grass and minor destruction behind. Anesko refused to lower the barrier until he knew for certain the army was gone, so Maren and Katori used their magic to see beyond the walls. They confirmed the enemy was indeed gone, and the barrier was removed.

The same day, a group of cloaked riders arrived, stirring up rumors around the school. It turned out to be the Assembly members, and surprisingly, Risod was among them. Maren and I joined Anesko for a meeting with them in the library, as there wasn't enough room in his chambers for all of us.

"I am glad to see that Risod is safe," I said, looking at her with concern. She was obviously exhausted, but her tired expression did little to mute her fierceness. She nodded her head in thanks.

"I am confused how you found her, though, considering you did not follow me to where the slayers held her captive." I kept my tone friendly and tried not to make the words sound like an accusation. Had they shown up, things would have gone much differently.

"I am sorry for deceiving you," Nemryth said. "I wanted to be sure you were not unknowingly leading us into a trap, and we waited to make our appearance. When we did, there was nothing but corpses waiting for us."

"The work of Erling's sorcerer, who is also his brother. Your aid would have been helpful, but I understand why you chose not to make your presence known immediately."

"I trust you have no ill feelings toward us?" she asked.

"No. Things worked out in the end. As well as can be expected, anyway."

Anesko cleared his throat. "Were you able to eliminate the rest of the dragon slayers?"

"As far as we know," Nemryth replied. "There weren't many left based on my count, but if any escaped, it would have only been one or two of them."

"Good. I am glad to be rid of at least one problem." Anesko leaned back against his chair and rubbed his temples.

"That is the reason we have come here. The more I consider their random appearance, the more I cannot believe that they came here accidentally. We must consider the possibility that they were scouts from a larger force. That, or they were sent here to find us specifically."

"What do you mean?" Anesko asked. "They knew who you are?"

"Risod said they interrogated her endlessly, wanting to know where the temple was, among other things. She is strong and told them nothing, but to answer your question, yes, they seemed to know who the Assembly was."

"I don't mean to sound rude, but how is that our problem?"

Nemryth's expression turned into a scowl for only a moment before she composed herself.

"If more of them come, then it will be your problem because they will hunt your dragons. The Order is already on the brink of disaster, and if the Order falls, all of dragon kind will be in danger."

Silence followed, and I heaved a sigh before speaking.

"The wild dragons are still here. Perhaps they have changed their mind about leaving."

"They haven't," Anesko said. "I spoke with Getarros this morning. They will be gone before the day is over. We cannot rely on them."

I had hoped they would stay, but I was not surprised. Dragons were stubborn creatures.

"If I may be so bold as to ask, will the Assembly support us when the king resumes his war?" I asked.

Anesko snapped his head around to look at me, his eyes wide with shock. I wasn't trying to step on his toes, but I wanted to know. After all I had done for them, it was the least they could do.

Nemryth smiled at me.

"Ages ago, we agreed to let our kind bond with yours. For a long time, I was disappointed in our decision, thinking that men were selfish and undeserving of the bond, yet I have come to see that is not true of all of you. The Assembly will support the Order, even in war."

"Thank you," Anesko said, bowing his head. "With our combined efforts, I have hope we will prevail against our enemies, wherever they come from."

"With that said, I have a request."

"Speak it."

"The Assembly has decided to be part of this world. We ask that you allow us to live here at the Citadel with you. It is long overdue for us to leave our temple."

"Granted," Anesko said without hesitation.

"Thank you. This is a new beginning."

I considered Anesko's words as I stood on the ramparts of the wall. They struck a chord within me, and I knew they rang truer than any of us could yet realize. With the Assembly on our side, I was just as confident as Anesko that we could overcome any adversity.

Perhaps that would eventually convince Getarros and the other wild dragons to change course and join the Order. Or perhaps we would find more dragons among the black-market traders. Or, to be even more hopeful, perhaps those who had previously provided dragons to the school would soon do so again.

Only time would reveal the next twist on our path, but I was determined to march forward with optimistic steps. I took a deep breath and stared into the distance, filled with a sense of hope and conviction. I was ready to fight for our future, and I would go to the ends of the world if I had to.

Whatever it takes, Sion said.

Whatever it takes, I replied.

THE END OF BOOK 14

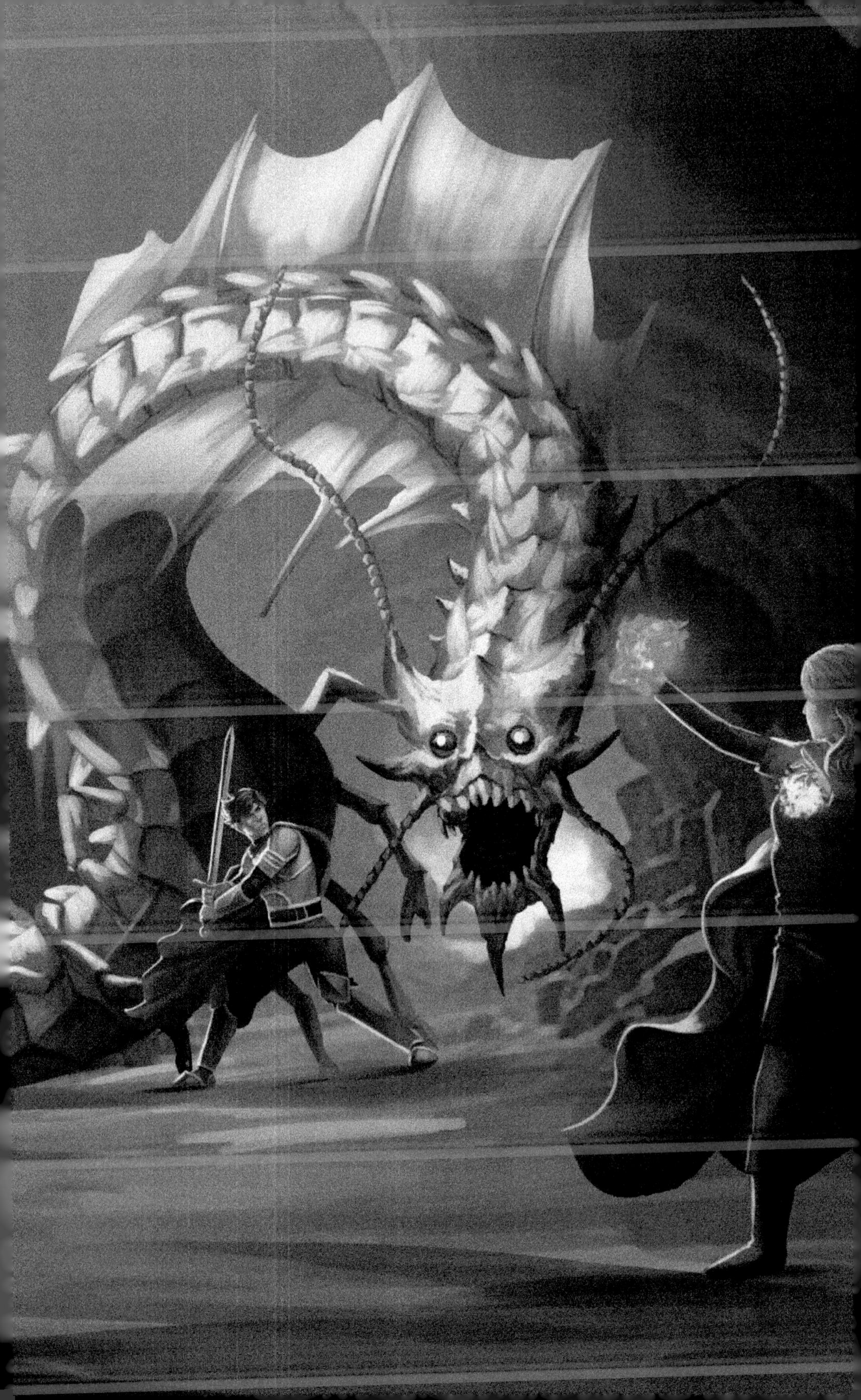

Tomb *of* Oaths

1

THE SUN CRESTED OVER THE horizon, bathing the landscape in a warm, golden glow. I stood atop a windswept cliff and watched the countryside come into sharp focus. Squinting against the sun, I stared into the distance. Master Anesko was late. He and a small group of riders had gone out to restock our supplies, but they'd yet to return.

Something wasn't right.

They should have returned yesterday. Under normal circumstances, it wouldn't be cause for concern, but recent times were anything but ordinary now that Shadamar had declared war on the Order.

While we tried to remain within the safety of the Citadel, there were times such as now when it was unavoidable. The wind picked up, tussling my hair and pulling at my cloak.

Do you see anything?

I glanced up at Sion, who wheeled lazily overhead in a wide circle.

Nothing, she replied.

I've got a bad feeling. Perhaps we should scout around to see if we can find any sign of them.

Sion landed gracefully beside me and snorted, thin tendrils of smoke rising from her nostrils.

If Shadamar has done something to them—

You'll flame them, I said, finishing her sentence.

Indeed.

I smiled and patted her gleaming red neck scales, then climbed up her shoulder and settled into the saddle. With a powerful flap of her wings, we were airborne, climbing into the clouds. The wind stung my face, but I relished the feeling of flight. Soaring through the sky, all my problems seemed… inconsequential. Temporarily, anyway.

Sion and I moved as one, banking and diving in effortless synchrony. We twisted through a narrow ravine, timing our movements perfectly to avoid the jagged walls. I leaned into each turn, feeling the pull of momentum. Sion responded to my subtle shifts of weight, angling her wings to ride the currents rising from the valley below. Our bond was strong, deeper than words could express.

As we burst from the ravine into the open sky, I scanned the area beneath us. There was no sign of Anesko or the others. Sion's determination to find them matched my own, our twin hearts beating as one, but it wasn't safe out here. Not alone. As if to prove that, Sion sniffed the air and growled.

We've got company.

I spotted them almost immediately coming from the south. A group of five riders. They didn't need to be closer for me to know they were Shadamar's men.

We're outnumbered. Get us back to the Citadel.

Sion's rage filled the bond. She wanted to fight, but common sense prevailed and she circled back, heading for the safety of the school. The king's riders took up pursuit. Sion tucked her wings closer to her body, gaining speed as we sped across the landscape. The dragons were quick, though, and they drew closer, the shouts of their riders carried by the wind.

Hold on, Sion said.

She issued a fierce roar and flapped her wings, propelling us forward with a burst of speed. I gripped the saddle as tightly as I could, my heart hammering with adrenaline. Sion was a powerful dragon, but even she had her limits, and her haste was short-lived.

The soldiers whooped with excitement as they gained on us. I clenched my jaw and silently urged Sion to go faster. We flew past the cliffs we'd been at shortly before and the Citadel came into view. Its grand towers and thick walls towered over everything around it, a beacon of protection.

We're almost there, I said. *We can make it.*

Sion let out a defiant growl, her wings beating with renewed vigor. The riders behind us were no longer closing the gap, but we weren't gaining ground. A horn blared, and I could see people scrambling along the parapets. If the king's riders were smart, they'd give up the chase before they got too close to the walls, but they weren't letting up.

If they open the barrier, the soldiers will get through behind us.

That would be foolish of them, Sion huffed, her focus on keeping up the frenzied pace.

Yes, unless... unless they don't intend to capture us. The realization suddenly struck me. Their orders might be to kill on sight. If that were the case, then it explained why they hadn't turned back. For them, the risk was worth the possible reward.

They will not harm you. I'll flame them from existence before they get close.

The confidence behind her words brought a smile to my lips. I leaned forward in the saddle and squeezed my legs against her, knowing what she aimed to do. With a final flap, she wrapped her wings around herself and barrel rolled.

Once, twice, three times. The world spun around me, a dizzying display of color. I felt more than saw the barrier recede, and then Sion leveled out and spread her wings wide, catching the air and quickly descending to the courtyard.

I looked back to see one of the royal riders slam into the barrier. The hole that was opened for Sion was already closed, and the dragon roared in anger and pain. The others swooped up in time to avoid colliding with the magical shield, temporarily blotting out the sun as they passed overhead.

Maren rushed down from the wall, taking the stairs two at a time.

"Are you all right?"

"I'm fine," I answered as I slid down Sion's shoulder. "That was close, but I wasn't expecting trouble."

"Where are the others?"

I shook my head. "They never arrived. It's not like Anesko to be late." I lowered my voice and glanced around to ensure no one was eavesdropping. "I think they might have been captured."

Maren's expression turned grave. "We need to inform the other Curates. If Shadamar has taken them, we're in trouble. Anesko knows all the secrets of the Citadel."

"He would never reveal them," I said.

"Not willingly, no, but my uncle has used his magic to break people before. I don't doubt he'll try the same tactics now."

"I'll gather the others. We should be prepared for the worst, but we also need to plan for the inevitable. The days of mourning are almost at an end."

2

THE COUNCIL ROOM WAS TOO warm. A fire burned low in the brazier, but it produced enough heat to make the space uncomfortable. I blinked several times, feeling drowsy. Almost all the other Curates had joined us, but we were waiting on Henrik.

I glanced around the table. They were all tired, their exhaustion evident by the look in their eyes. Despite that, they carried on. Would any of them bend under the weight of another problem? I hoped not. We were sorely outnumbered as it was, and although the Assembly pledged to aid us, I feared it would not be enough.

The door swung open and Henrik stepped inside. "Sorry," he grunted. "I had a few things to finish."

"No need to apologize," I said. "We're all overburdened. This will be quick."

He took a seat, and I looked at Maren. She nodded, indicating I should be the one to break the news. I cleared my throat and stood.

"As you are all aware, Master Anesko and the others have not returned. Sion and I did some scouting, but there was no sign of them. I believe they may have been captured by Shadamar."

No one moved or said anything, but the silence told me all I needed to know. Finally, Master Katori spoke.

"Have you tried to reach him by magical means?"

"I tried a few times," Maren answered. "Each time, I encountered something blocking me. My uncle is a powerful sorcerer, so it would be a simple task for him to block my magic. I'm with Eldwin on this. I think Anesko has been captured."

"This poses several problems, especially since Anesko knows things about the Citadel that no one else does." I glanced at each of the Curates in turn. "We're running low on supplies, and there are only a few days left before Shadamar marches his army back to our gates. Even if Anesko isn't being held prisoner, we need a plan."

"This is the last thing we need," Curate Mila said. She had been the one to replace Curate Josephine after her betrayal. Thinking back on that reminded me of the battle against the False King. It felt as though that had been an eternity ago.

"It is not ideal, but we've faced worse."

"Have we?" Mila huffed. "Things look pretty dire right now. I gave up my family for the Order, and now it seems that I will die for my decision."

"I, too, know what it means to sacrifice for the Order," Maren said. "It is my uncle who seeks our destruction, after all."

Mila's face flushed pink. "Yes, I know. Forgive my outburst. I'm tired."

"We all are," Maren replied soothingly. "These are difficult times at best."

I nodded in agreement. "Yes, we do not face the best odds, but I am sure we will prevail." I hoped my words sounded more confident than I felt. "Let us tackle one problem at a time. We will need supplies to outlast a siege. It will be risky, but we need to send a few groups out to get what we need. Curate Henrik, can you organize that?"

"Yes," he answered.

"Good. Whoever goes outside these walls must understand the danger, and they must return before the days of mourning are over."

Henrik nodded.

"The next issue is the barrier." The eyes of several Curates widened. I raised a hand to silence their fears. "It is secure, but we must be prepared if anything happens to it. As Maren said, Shadamar is a powerful sorcerer. I think we should shorten the shifts of those who are lending their energy to power it. If there is any weakness at all, Shadamar will find it. Master Katori, I trust you will handle that?"

"Of course."

"Thank you. We may be outnumbered, but that makes us fiercer than Shadamar's men. We have everything to lose, but they do not."

"I have an idea," Maren said. All eyes turned to her, including mine. "I know this may sound crazy, but I think we should request aid from Valgaard."

I blinked in surprise, then immediately frowned.

"We haven't heard from Valgaard since Hrodin was imprisoned for his treachery," Henrik said, speaking exactly what I was thinking. "None of our letters have been replied to."

"I'm aware of that, which is why I think we need to go there in person. I volunteer myself, since it is my idea."

"Not alone, you won't," I said. "I'm coming with you."

Katori steepled her fingers and spoke up. "We should not weaken our defenses on a whim. Who knows if the riders of Valgaard will greet you warmly or with chains? I do not think this is wise."

"It may be dangerous, but if they join us, we are stronger, and the benefits outweigh the risks."

"And if they kill you on sight, we become weaker," Katori replied.

I didn't disagree with Katori, but Maren had a point. We desperately needed help, and Valgaard was a possible answer to our dilemma.

"Master Katori outranks us all, but I think we should vote on this. I vote yes. Maren and I will go to Valgaard to seek aid. If you agree, raise your hand."

Unsurprisingly, Katori did not lift hers, but many of the Curates did.

"It is settled, then. Maren and I will leave as soon as possible. With any luck, we'll bring an army back with us. Do we need to discuss anything else?" I looked at Maren, who shook her head. None of the Curates said anything. "Very well. Let's get to it, then."

After the others were gone, I sat down and looked at Maren. "What makes you think Valgaard will help us?"

"They are prideful people. If they want to make things right, this is their opportunity. And with Hrodin out of the picture, I think it'll be easier to sway them."

"I suppose you may be right. Hopefully, no one wants to marry you this time."

Maren laughed. It had been a while since I'd heard that sound, and it brought a grin to my face.

"I'm already taken by a good man, so I would be forced to pass." Maren glanced at the door, then lowered her voice, her expression turning serious. "I've been thinking…"

"Yes?"

"Whether Valgaard agrees to help or not, there is another that could help us, but…"

"But what?"

"I don't know if things would go as planned."

"I don't understand. Who else is there?"

"Midia."

3

"OUR ENEMY?" I STARED AT her, stunned.

"Osnen's enemy, but yes. There's a saying I'm sure you've heard. 'The enemy of my enemy is my friend.'"

"But... they—"

"The Necromancer and the False King did those things, Eldwin. What they did to your father was evil, but the common people of Midia did not commit those atrocities."

"Maybe not, but they allowed them to happen."

"If they did, it was because they were under duress. You know as well as I do that the False King forced his will onto them."

What she said was true, but I didn't care. The False King was one man. If the people had stood against him, they could have stopped him. I turned those thoughts aside.

"Why do you say it wouldn't go as planned?"

Maren sighed. "They are at odds with Osnen. Or rather, the leadership of Osnen. If they were given the opportunity to defeat Shadamar and end my family's line, I fear they might try to take the throne. That could plunge our lands into worse chaos than we already see now."

Her words hung heavy in the air. The thought of seeking aid from Midia wasn't something I would have ever considered, but desperate times called for desperate measures. I supposed if there was even a slim chance that they could be convinced to join our cause against Shadamar, it was a risk we should take.

"Why didn't you mention it to the others?" I asked.

"Katori was already against going to Valgaard, and if you have uneasy feelings about Midia, imagine how everyone else will feel about it."

Images of the battle flashed in my mind's eye and I clenched my jaw, trying to weigh the consequences of what Maren was proposing.

"If we are to consider reaching out to the people of Midia, we must tread carefully. We cannot afford to let our guard down or be blinded by false promises."

"I agree," Maren said. "We will make our intentions clear, as well as the consequences should they betray us. The wounds of the past run deep, and we don't need more war in our lands. We need peace."

I nodded. "If you are set on this path, then I will trust your judgment. Midia is closer, but I think we should go to Valgaard first. If anything happens while we're gone, it'll give us the option of coming back here first before traveling into more dangerous territory."

"That was my thought as well."

Maren and I made preparations for our journey, ensuring we had enough supplies for the long flight ahead. I also made sure to grab thick coats to ward off Valgaard's freezing weather. As I saddled Sion, the weight of our mission settled heavily on my shoulders. The fate of the Order hung in the balance, and we were going to seek the aid of our enemies.

Enemies may become allies, Sion said, sensing my brooding thoughts.

I know, but our decisions are made from desperation. The choices we make could well determine the course of our future.

That is a good thing. If you can gain some control over what the future holds, it is better than leaving everything to chance.

I tightened the straps under Sion's belly and rubbed her scales affectionately. Henrik and Katori joined us in the stables to say goodbye. It was a somber parting, filled with uncertainty.

"Safe travels," Henrik said. "I expect to see you back here in a few days."

"And I expect to see this place still standing when I get back," I replied, offering as much of a grin as I could muster, considering my words.

"We will await your return," Katori said softly.

I nodded and looked to where Maren was saddling Demris. She finished with the straps and climbed up his shoulder and into the saddle. She nodded, and I urged Sion to take the lead. She leaped into the air and flew in a wide circle around the Citadel. There was no sign of the royal riders from earlier.

A section of the barrier faded, giving us our exit. Sion bolted through the hole, and Demris followed directly behind us. We turned west and flew at a quick pace. Although time was a precious commodity, there was no sense in exhausting ourselves.

Dense forests and rolling hills passed below us, and I found myself thinking about Maren's proposition regarding Midia. It seemed too risky of a move, but with Valgaard's support uncertain, we needed all the options we could get. The thought crossed my mind that Valgaard and Midia could unite against us, eliminating both the Order and the crown.

Don't be foolish, Sion said.

I know it isn't likely, but given our luck, it wouldn't surprise me.

We flew for a few hours before landing in an open field to give Sion and Demris time to rest. A stream flowed nearby, and Maren and I sat on its bank, stretching our legs. We remained silent, but her presence offered comfort that I found nowhere else except within my bond with Sion. My love for each of them was distinct, but they were equal in intensity.

"What if we get there only to find the place abandoned?" I asked. "That would explain the lack of communication from them."

"Hrodin was stubborn, as his people are. I'm sure they just refuse to respond."

"Perhaps." I wrapped my maimed arm around her and pulled her close, resting my head on her shoulder. I longed for the day that peace was restored. Maren and I had yet to talk about bringing children into this world, and while I wanted that, I knew it wasn't safe to. Not yet, anyway.

There will always be evil in this world, Sion said thoughtfully. *You must not be afraid to forge a family because of that.*

You and Maren are all the family I need right now. And what of you? Will you decide to lay an egg or two?

One day, though not anytime soon. I am still young, you know.

That's the ideal time to have children for humans. If we wait too long, it becomes impossible.

Dragons are not fragile like humans, Sion replied. She stomped over to the stream and drank of the water, then nuzzled my back, wiping her wet snout on me.

Come on. Let us see what awaits us at Valgaard.

4

I DON'T REMEMBER IT BEING this cold, I complained, shivering violently against the biting wind and snow.

I do, but the cold cannot dim my flames.

Sion opened her jaws and spewed forth a torrent of fire. The warmth briefly pushed away the chill, but it returned quickly, feeling colder than before. The thick coat I brought offered little protection, but it was better than nothing. The air grew thinner the higher we flew, and Sion struggled to breathe properly.

After what felt like an eternity, Valgaard became visible as a dark blotch among the blanket of white. It sat upon the natural plateau of a mountainside that overlooked a long line of jagged peaks. It was impossible to see much of anything else because of the heavy snowfall, but Sion and Demris landed without incident.

The dragons trudged around the school to the enormous cave that was set in the mountainside, their footsteps muffled by the thick banks of snow. We stepped into the cave and the familiar network of honeycomb openings greeted us, though there were no dragons visible. I dismounted and enjoyed the warmth that radiated from the walls.

"It's been a long time s-since we've been h-here," I stuttered, glancing around as I furiously rubbed my hands together. Everything looked the same, but it was too quiet.

Do you sense any other dragons?

No, Sion replied. *The caves are deserted.*

I looked at Maren. "Sion says there are no d-dragons here. We may have come all this way f-for nothing."

"Let's check the school," she said.

Stay here with Demris. Let me know if you find anything.

I grabbed Maren's hand, and we stepped back out into the cold. The frosty air clung to my lungs, making each breath feel heavy and labored. We marched toward the entrance, our feet sinking with each step, and we left behind a trail of footprints. We reached the massive doors, their steel surface covered in a thick layer of frost. I gripped one of the handles and pulled, but the door wouldn't budge.

"Stand back," Maren said.

I moved out of the way, and she lifted her right hand, uttering a string of words. The ground rumbled briefly, and the door slowly opened to reveal a dark entryway. When we first visited Valgaard, a rider named Kell greeted us. He'd led us through this same doorway, and torches had burned brightly, lighting the way.

Now, there was only darkness.

Sion could feel my unease in the bond. *What's wrong?*

Nothing, I replied. *At least, I don't think so. We're about to go inside, but it seems empty, just like the stable.*

Perhaps they disbanded after Hrodin's treachery.

We'll find out soon enough.

Instinctively, I drew my sword and took the lead, stepping into the great hall. "Can you do something about the gloom?" I asked Maren, looking over my shoulder.

A globe of floating light burst into existence overhead, illuminating the interior of the hall. It was just as bare and cold as our last visit. I walked ahead, my eyes darting left and right, my senses on high alert.

The hall opened into a large room, and against the center wall was the throne. It was empty. A foul smell drifted on the air, and I buried my nose in my elbow.

"What is that stench?"

"Over there," Maren said.

I looked at her. She was pointing to a fireplace. Unearthly green flames flickered within it, but my attention was instantly diverted to a hunched figure sitting on the floor in front of the fire. Its back was to us, and the smell got worse as I drew closer. I used the flat of my blade to tap the figure on the shoulder, suspecting it was a corpse.

It was not.

The figure shifted and rose to its feet, towering a full foot taller than me. I brought my sword up defensively and retreated to Maren's side. A ball of flame formed between her hands, but she didn't attack the figure.

"Who is there?"

The voice sounded normal, but as the figure turned to face us, I saw the terrible truth. It appeared to be human, but its face was misshapen and looked like a strange mix between a man and an animal. I pointed the tip of my sword at the creature.

"Don't come any closer," I said.

"I mean you no harm," it replied, holding its hand up in a gesture of surrender. Its eyes, a vibrant shade of blue, held a glimmer of intelligence despite its appearance. Two horns rose from its temples, extending several inches.

"What is that thing?" I looked at Maren as if she might know the answer.

"I have no idea."

"I am no *thing*," the creature snapped. "I am a man, cursed with this appearance."

"Cursed how?" I asked.

"Tell me your names first. This is my home, and you've come in uninvited."

Before I could protest, Maren said, "I am Maren, and this is Eldwin."

"Maren Toft? And Eldwin Baines? I know your names well."

Silence ensued, and judging by the tone of its voice, I assumed the man-beast did not view us in a positive light.

"What happened here?" Maren asked. "Where are the dragons? And the riders?"

"It is a long story."

"We're a bit short on time, so make it quick," I said.

Maren cast a glare at me and turned back to the creature. "He is right. We are short on time, but I am interested in hearing your tale."

The man-beast sighed, his eyes full of sorrow and frustration. The green flames in the fireplace crackled, casting an eerie glow on the creature's twisted features.

"Long ago, when the Order first came to our lands, we fought against them and their rules. We lost the battle, and in our time of weakness, a powerful *volur* came to our aid. She convinced the Order not to slay us, and they reluctantly agreed. In return for her help, my ancestor swore an oath to her.

"He promised to live with honor despite being forced to adapt to the changing world around us. Knowing he was too prideful for his own good, the *volur* wanted to ensure he would fulfill his oath long after she was gone. She told him if his bloodline ever forsook the oath, a terrible curse would befall Valgaard. As you know, the oath was broken."

"Who broke the oath?" I asked.

"My father did," the man-beast said. "Hrodin."

5

"You're Hrodin's son?" I exclaimed.

I didn't know the former schoolmaster had a son, though it made sense he would. He viewed himself as a king, so he would want an heir to carry on his lineage.

"Yes," the man-beast replied. "I am Bryngar, the heir to the throne of Valgaard. When my father succumbed to his greed and lust for power, he broke the sacred oath that bound our bloodline to the *volur.*" He waved a hand at his appearance. "This curse is a reflection of our family's betrayal."

"I don't understand," Maren said. "How does this relate to the disappearance of your dragons and riders?"

"My father brought dishonor to our people, and they do not feel we are worthy of calling Valgaard home. They left. I am all that remains."

It was obvious Bryngar was not a threat. I sheathed my sword. "Why didn't you go with them? Why stay behind?"

"I am not worthy to be among my people."

"You didn't break the oath," Maren scoffed. "Your father did. And he is suffering his just reward in prison."

"I am not innocent," Bryngar said. "After the Assembly took him, I tried to find him to break him free. I did not realize…" he paused and waved a clawed hand. "I did not realize the gravity of what he had done."

"Did you find him?"

"No."

"Then you technically did nothing wrong," Maren said.

"There is more. Before I understood the truth, I sent a message to our brethren far across the sea. Unlike those of us here at Valgaard, they do not have a love for dragons."

"The dragon slayers," I whispered, looking at Maren.

"Yes. I summoned them… to kill the Assembly."

"You did what?" Maren took a step forward, the ball of flame between her hands crackling with her anger.

"My father lied about why he agreed to help the dark rider Kage. I thought he was just in his intentions, but now I know better. I am sorry, though I know that does not mean much."

Maren dispelled the fire, but fury burned within her eyes. "You need to call them off. The Assembly are our allies."

"I tried, but they do not answer to me. Once they find out there are other dragons in Osnen besides the Assembly, they will bring their full might."

"They already know. They tried to kill me and Sion."

Bryngar cast his gaze to the floor. "I cannot undo what I have wrought, but I will do what I can to make amends."

"You won't be able to go anywhere looking like that," I said. "You'll be hunted like an animal."

"How can you break the curse?" Maren asked. "There must be a way."

"There is a way, but I cannot do it."

"Why not? You said you would do whatever you can to make amends."

"And I will, but I cannot do this because I am forbidden to enter the *volur's* resting place. Her magic prevents it."

Maren looked at me, and I knew what she was thinking despite her lack of words. I nodded my head slightly, so she knew I was with her.

"I must tell you why we have come here," Maren said, turning her attention back to Bryngar. "The king of Osnen, my uncle, seeks to destroy the Citadel and all who dwell there. Knowing him, he won't stop there. He'll come here next, intent upon slaughtering any rider who does not swear fealty to him. We do not have the strength to combat his armies, and we came here seeking aid. If we break your curse, will you help us?"

"Even if I didn't look the way I do now, I would still offer my assistance. My father's actions were unjust, and the people of Valgaard will stand with you. I will need to rally them, but it will be a difficult task looking like this. If you break the curse, I will go to them. They will be relieved to know there is a way to regain their lost honor."

"How do we break the curse?" I asked.

"It will not be easy. You will need to enter the *volur's* burial chamber and place an amulet around her neck. Once that is done, the curse should lift."

I shrugged. "That sounds fairly easy to me."

"Powerful enchantments and traps guard her resting place. It is a treacherous journey, even for capable riders such as yourselves."

"Where is her tomb?" Maren asked.

"It is within the mountain. The entrance is inside the stable. I can give you a map, but I cannot tell you where the traps are. No one has been down there since she was laid to rest."

Maren nodded. "And the amulet? I trust you have it?"

"I can get it," Bryngar answered.

"Will our dragons be able to come with us?" I asked.

"I don't think so. The tunnels are said to be narrow."

Maren and I stared at one another for a moment in silence. She was a powerful sorcerer, and I had no doubts that she could disable the wards protecting the burial chamber, but we were going in blind. She stepped close to me and lowered her voice.

"We need their help."

"I know," I replied. "But we need to hurry. If Shadamar returns before we get back, there may be nothing left to come home to."

"We will do it," Maren said, turning to look at Bryngar.

"Thank you." Bryngar lowered his head in a bow. "I will get the amulet and the map. Please, eat and drink while you wait. All that is mine is at your service."

He left the room, and I waited a moment to ensure he was gone before I spoke. "Did you hear what he said? More dragon slayers will be coming."

"I heard him, but we have more pressing problems right now. One at a time, if you don't mind." She smiled and leaned in to kiss me. My lips met hers, and I wrapped my arms around her, embracing her tightly.

"You're right. Let's focus on breaking this curse."

6

AFTER BRYNGAR RETRIEVED THE MAP and amulet, he led us out to the stable. Sion and Demris had curled up in their own caves, and Sion regarded Bryngar curiously.

He is human, but magic masks his true appearance.

Yes, he is cursed because of what Hrodin did. Maren and I are going to break the curse for him. In return, Valgaard will help us against Shadamar. You and Demris will stay behind because the tunnel is too narrow for you to fit.

Sion growled with displeasure, but when Bryngar mentioned he would feed them while we were gone, that eased her irritation.

"This way," he said.

We left the main chamber and followed him deeper into the mountain, going beyond the hatchery where I had first seen a dragon egg. Bryngar stopped at a large, circular iron door embedded in the wall. It was engraved with ancient symbols.

"Beyond this door lies the entrance to the *volur's* burial chamber," Bryngar said, his voice tinged with solemnity. "It has remained undisturbed for centuries. Be cautious and tread lightly."

"We will," Maren replied.

Bryngar pulled the door open, and Maren stepped into the gloom. Her globe of light followed, bobbing lightly as it traveled through the air. I rested my hand on the hilt of my sword and walked across the threshold, briefly wondering if Bryngar was sending us to our deaths.

"I will leave the door open for your return."

"We appreciate that," I said, his words soothing my sudden distrust. "We'll be back soon."

Maren and I walked side by side. The tunnel was long, and the shadows beyond Maren's light made it feel as though it stretched into eternity. There was a heavy silence, and the air felt stale. Faded murals on the walls depicted dragons in flight and epic battles. Maren's globe cast eerie shadows, making the scenes come to life in a ghostly dance.

Our footsteps echoed off the walls, breaking the silence and making me feel as if we were intruders treading on sacred ground.

"I can feel ancient magic emanating from… everywhere," Maren whispered. "She must have been powerful indeed."

"Do you sense any wards?"

"Yes. There is one up ahead."

I nodded and admired the paintings on the walls as we walked.

As we approached the ward, I noticed a shift in the atmosphere. The air grew charged with an otherworldly energy, crackling with power that sent a shiver down my spine. Maren pulled back on my hand.

"There it is."

Of course, I didn't see anything, but I released her hand and took a step back. She raised her hands, and the globe of light dimmed slightly as she focused her magic.

"It's an intricate web of enchantments," she said. "This is going to take me some time."

While I waited for her to break the ward, I studied one of the murals. It depicted a valiant rider atop a dragon, his sword raised triumphantly. A strange creature I'd never seen before lay on the ground, slain. I traced my finger along the lines of the picture and wondered how many stories of the past were lost in time.

I glanced back at Maren. Her brow was furrowed in concentration, and a few beads of sweat glistened on her forehead, evidence of the strain she was enduring to undo the enchantments. With a final surge of power, Maren broke the ward. I saw the air ripple faintly, and Maren's shoulders slumped.

"That was strong, even after all this time."

"You don't look so good. Do you need to rest for a moment?"

Maren inhaled a deep breath and shook her head. "I'm fine. That just took more effort than I expected."

"Take my arm," I offered, linking her arm with mine and supporting her weight as we continued ahead. She leaned on me, her exhaustion evident with every step. The tunnel seemed to stretch on endlessly. The air grew colder, and a chill settled within my bones. I shivered and pulled my cloak tighter.

Reaching a three-pronged fork, we paused and Maren looked at the map Bryngar gave us.

"Which way do we go?" I asked.

"The map only shows one tunnel in this area, so I'm not sure. Am I looking at this right?"

Maren handed the map to me. I held it out flat under the bobbing light and inspected it. Judging by the distance we had walked so far, she was right. In fact, there wasn't a three-pronged fork anywhere on the map.

"I see the same thing you do."

"Maybe Bryngar gave us the wrong map."

"Or maybe he's deceived us," I said. "He seemed too willing to help, don't you think?"

"I think he is sincere. Hrodin may have led him astray initially, but Bryngar wants to do what is right now that he knows the truth. He said no one has ever been down here before, so maybe whoever laid the sorceress to rest didn't map the way correctly on purpose."

"That's a fair guess. It's up to us to figure out which path is the right one, then." I nodded to the path on the left. "Do you sense anything down this one?"

Maren shook her head. "No. Just these two."

"Then I think it's safe to say we can skip this one. If there are no wards, there shouldn't be anything to protect."

"That was my thought as well," Maren said. "Which one should we try first?"

I studied the two remaining paths before us. The path to the right was narrower and the floor was uneven, while the one in the middle appeared wider and smoother. My instincts told me the middle path was the one we should take. I pointed to the one in the middle.

"This one seems like more effort was taken to craft it, so I think this is the correct one."

"That makes sense to me," Maren replied. "Let's see where it goes."

We ventured ahead, continuing down the main tunnel. As we walked, I couldn't shake off a sense of foreboding that settled over me like a heavy cloak. There was something about the air down here that felt different—an almost tangible presence that made the hairs on the back of my neck stand on end.

"Something isn't right," I mumbled. I drew my sword and stepped in front of Maren. The globe of light illuminated the tunnel ahead by at least a dozen paces, and there was nothing out of the ordinary in sight. I took a step forward, then another, expecting the light to reveal some ghastly creature, but there was nothing.

"Maybe I'm just imagining—" With my next step, my foot sank into the ground. A metallic sound echoed through the air, and the floor gave way beneath me.

7

For a brief moment, I was weightless.

And then my stomach churned as I fell. I stared in terrified disbelief, but before I fell too far, I stopped mid-air. Glancing up, I saw Maren's face twisted in concentration. I slowly rose until I was on the ledge beside her.

"Thanks," I said, suddenly feeling warm and sweaty. "That was close." I sheathed my blade.

"You're welcome." She smiled weakly.

"You should sit down. I know we don't have much time, but you need to rest. Your face is pale."

Maren nodded, not bothering to argue. We retreated to where the tunnel branched and sat down on the ground. Maren leaned back against the wall and closed her eyes. The glow from the orb above cast its soft aura over her, enhancing her natural beauty.

I watched her for a moment, concern gnawing at my insides. Maren was always the strong one, the one who carried us through the toughest of situations with unwavering determination. Seeing her like this, drained and fatigued, made me realize just how much it had taken for her to break those enchantments.

She had pushed herself too hard. It was my turn to be the pillar of strength, to guide us through whatever lay ahead. I turned my attention to the map again. As I studied the worn parchment, a thought occurred to me.

"What if the path without wards is the correct way ahead?"

"What do you mean?" Maren asked, her eyes still closed.

"I assumed the tunnels were protected by magic for a reason, but what if the opposite is true? What if the wards were put there to trick potential thieves into *thinking* there is something worth protecting?"

A smile crept across Maren's lips, and she cracked her eyes open. "You're brilliant sometimes, you know that?"

"I try."

We both laughed, and Maren leaned forward. She reached out and traced her finger along the lines of the map.

"If that's the case, then we've been going about this the wrong way. We need to take the path to the left. Help me up."

I stood and pulled her to her feet. "Are you feeling well enough to continue? We can leave and come back later. Bryngar left the door open for us."

"I can manage. My strength is slowly returning."

"Are you sure?"

"Yes. Come on." As if to prove her words, she strode past me. I hurried to catch up, and as we entered the tunnel, we slowed our pace. It never hurt to be cautious. After all, we could still be wrong about the traps.

"Here, let me check for more pressure plates," I said, pulling my sword back out and pushing the tip against the stones. Thankfully, none of them budged. We traversed the tunnel without incident and came around a bend that opened to another fork. Again, the map did not show the fork. Maren extended her senses, and we took the path that didn't have any wards.

Having solved the puzzle of the tunnels, we pressed on and reached the end of the labyrinth without any further obstacles. The temperature continued to drop as we journeyed deeper, and when we finally emerged from the tunnel, I understood why. Enormous chunks of glacial blue ice greeted us, forming a maze. The air was crisp, and I could see my breath as I exhaled. It was as if the very essence of winter had taken residence here. Maren's globe of light flickered, casting elongated shadows across the ice walls.

"This is incredible," Maren said, her voice filled with awe. Tiny clouds formed in front of her face as she breathed. I nodded wordlessly in agreement. The place felt almost otherworldly, as if we had stumbled upon a realm reserved for the gods. But there was no time for admiration; our task wasn't over yet. The map indicated we needed to navigate the frozen maze.

"The sorceress's body is on the other end of this," Maren said. "Magic is vibrating all around us, so watch your step and don't touch anything. I'll lead us from here."

Maren's steps were deliberate and measured, her focus on the path ahead. She seemed to have an innate understanding of this place, as if she could decipher its secrets by mere intuition. I mirrored her movements, trying to match her grace as we weaved through the intricate network of frozen corridors.

The maze seemed to stretch on endlessly. Neither of us spoke, and the silence that enveloped us felt almost palpable, broken only by the soft crunching of our boots on the icy floor. Suddenly, Maren came to a halt. I followed her gaze and saw what had caught her attention: a tomb of ice and stone covered in intricate symbols.

"That is her resting place," Maren said, breaking the silence.

I approached the tomb cautiously, my eyes scanning the intricate symbols etched into its icy surface. The surrounding air seemed to crackle with magic, and a surge of apprehension coursed through me. This was no ordinary tomb.

Maren gestured for me to stand back as she raised her hands, her fingers delicately tracing the patterns on the tomb. A soft chant escaped her lips, a melody that echoed throughout the cavern. Slowly, the ice melted away to reveal the stone beneath.

As the last vestiges of ice dissipated, a soft glow emanated from within the tomb. Maren reached out and pushed open the stone lid, revealing the skeletal remains of the sorceress. The tattered remnants of a robe covered the bones, and a metal tiara adorned her skull. It was obvious she had been laid to rest with reverence.

This woman had once wielded immense power, and now all that remained were fragile bones and a forgotten legacy. It was a reminder that no matter how much power one held; death was inevitable.

"We return this gift to you," Maren whispered. "The oath was broken, but it shall be restored."

With a somber finality, Maren carefully placed the amulet onto the sorceress's chest, right above where her heart would have once been.

"This should satisfy the curse. Can you close it back up?"

I nodded and heaved the stone lid back into place, then brushed my hands off. "Well, that wasn't too difficult."

"Not at all," Maren replied sarcastically, turning to look at me.

"If you don't count almost falling into oblivion, then this was probably the least dangerous thing we've done in a while."

The sound of sloshing water made me pause, and Maren looked beyond me. Her expression morphed from mild curiosity to dread. I swallowed hard and mouthed 'What is it?' but she wasn't paying me any attention. I grabbed the hilt of my blade and slowly turned around.

8

"Gods," I whispered in awe.

One of the ice walls had mostly melted, revealing a gigantic insect-like creature. It writhed on the ground as it struggled to get free of the remaining ice.

"She must have hidden something in her tomb to trigger the release of that thing," Maren said.

"What is it?"

"I don't know, but we should get out of here before it gets loose."

The chunk of ice cracked, and the creature was free. I stood in terror as it rose from the ground. The beast was easily ten feet long, and its segmented body had dozens of legs. It had leathery wings that were too small to use for flight, and long antennae extended from the tips of its head, each reaching several feet in length. Its icy blue chitinous exoskeleton glistened under Maren's globe of light. Sharp mandibles clicked together, emitting an eerie sound. Horns lined its back from its neck to its tail, and they glowed red with an inner fire.

Maren laid a hand on my arm, and the creature's antennae twitched, sensing our movements. Steam escaped from its fanged maw as it let out a bone-chilling roar, the sound reverberating through the cavern. It scrambled forward, leaving a trail of gouges on the stone floor. I pushed Maren behind me and brandished my sword, charging forward to meet the creature.

I slashed horizontally with my blade, aiming for the beast's underbelly. It recoiled, deflecting my assault with its armored hide. Intense pain flared up my arm, and I screamed, dropping my sword. The creature hissed a breath of scalding steam, narrowly missing me. Undeterred, it lunged, its mandibles snapping powerfully.

Magic crackled behind me, and a wave of flames rushed past, crashing into the beast. I scrambled backward on all fours, reaching Maren. She threw another blast of flames, and I watched as they swept over the creature with no effect.

"Try to freeze it!" I shouted.

Maren extended her hands, eyes narrowed in concentration, and a surge of frost burst forth, swirling around the creature. The temperature dropped even further, but the ice did nothing to injure the creature. It simply melted. Maren's brow creased with her frustration.

We needed a new plan. As the creature advanced, I racked my brain. There had to be a weakness, a vulnerability we could exploit. Maren tugged my arm, leading me around the tomb and behind an ice wall.

"My magic is useless against that thing," she huffed.

"When I struck it, my arm burned like fire." I peeked out from the side of the wall and the creature sprinted toward our position.

"Get down!" I threw Maren to the ground, covering her with my body. The beast slammed into the wall, shattering the ice. Its momentum carried it past us, and I hurried to my feet, pulling Maren up and dragging her toward a narrow passage on the other side of the tomb. The beast turned around. Its claws scraped against the stone floor as it readied itself for another attack.

I came to an abrupt halt as the passage ended, leaving us with nowhere to go. Panic threatened to paralyze me, but I clenched my jaw and pushed the feeling aside with every ounce of strength I could summon.

"What do we do?" Maren asked.

"It's not invincible," I replied, though I found it difficult to believe my own words. "There must be some way to kill it. I don't understand why your ice didn't work. The thing was frozen."

"She must have used a spell I don't know of to trap it."

"What other spells can you use? We know fire and ice don't work."

"I know many, but I don't think magic alone is going to help us. We need to be coordinated about this."

An idea came to me. "The antennae on its head. Maybe if we damage them, it will immobilize it, at least long enough to escape."

"We can't leave that thing alive in here. What if it gets out? It would rampage through the school. No, we need to kill it."

She was right. If it could smash through a solid wall of ice, there was no telling what else it could do.

"We could crush it," I suggested. "I can draw its attention while you use magic to pin it between the ice walls."

"I like that, but I've got a better idea. I'll bring the ceiling down on it."

"You're going to destroy the cavern? I don't like the idea of disrupting the sorceress's grave. We could cause something worse than Bryngar's curse if we do."

"No, I'm not going to destroy it. I'll just collapse part of the ceiling, enough to crush the creature and seal the tomb."

"I don't have a better idea," I said. "What do you need me to do?"

"Distract it, but don't die."

The hint of a smile played at her lips, and I leaned in and gave her a quick kiss.

"If I die, I'll just haunt you as a spirit," I said with a chuckle.

"Funny. We'll need it to be near the end of the maze. I'll get into position, and you draw it toward me."

I nodded. "I'll grab my sword and lure it to the far side of the cavern while you make a run for it. Let me know when you're ready, and I'll bring it your way."

Maren placed her right hand on my face, softly caressing my cheek while she stared into my eyes. "I love you, Eldwin."

"I love you, too."

She pressed her lips to mine, and I returned her kiss, drinking in the moment. I prayed this wasn't the end for us. Maren broke away and playfully shoved me ahead of her. Backtracking to where we entered the passage, I risked a glance into the cavern. There was no sign of the creature. I took a deep breath and silently counted, preparing myself. Nodding at Maren, I sprinted into the chamber and made a beeline for my sword.

A blur of blue color zipped overhead, dropping in front of me. The creature hissed, its mandibles snapping menacingly. I skidded to a halt, narrowly avoiding its scalding breath. It lunged at me, claws outstretched, but I sidestepped to the right and threw myself forward, tumbling to the ground beside its legs.

The beast skittered around, one of its legs grazing my left arm while another kicked my sword, sending it spinning just out of reach. Blood welled up from the shallow wound.

"Eldwin!" Maren yelled from across the chamber.

I rolled away and grabbed my sword, scrambling to my feet. "Go!"

Maren was a blur in my periphery as she ran toward the maze of ice walls. I kept my gaze on the creature, ensuring it didn't go after her. My body tremored, both from the cold and the adrenaline pumping through my veins. I tightened my grip on the hilt of my blade, the weight of it in my hand providing a small measure of comfort.

I needed to buy Maren enough time to prepare her spell. I jabbed the tip of my sword at the creature, not intending to land a strike. It hissed again and dodged my attack, moving faster than its size should have allowed, its body lithe and fluid. I cursed under my breath, knowing I was in over my head.

A flash of light pulsed from the maze, and I took that as my sign that Maren was in place. With a silent prayer to the gods, I darted toward the maze. I navigated through its twisting paths, constantly changing direction in an attempt to confuse the creature, but its heavy footfalls grew louder behind me with every second.

I spotted Maren at the end of the maze, her hands raised. They were glowing with a pulsing azure light, casting an ethereal glow on the ice walls. I closed the distance and ran past her, turning in time to see the creature barreling straight for her. Maren unleashed her spell, sending a wave of magical energy into the ceiling.

A thunderous *crack* echoed through the cavern, and an enormous chunk of stone broke off, falling directly on top of the beast. The deafening crash echoed through the chamber and the creature was crushed beneath the stone's weight. A few smaller stones tumbled down, and then there was nothing but silence.

Time passed slowly as we waited for a sign of success. Suddenly, a bright molten substance leaked out from beneath the stone. It was hot enough to liquefy the stone and even melt some of the nearby ice.

"You did it," I said.

Maren turned to face me with a weak smile before her eyes rolled back into her head and she collapsed.

9

I RUSHED TO HER SIDE, checking for the rhythm of her heartbeat. It was weak, but steady. I sheathed my sword and lifted her off the ground, throwing her over my shoulder. The wound on my arm throbbed, but I pushed through the discomfort and made my way through the tunnel, carefully following the map to guide me back to safety.

As promised, Bryngar had left the door open, and I returned to the caves where Sion and Demris were resting. Maren was still unconscious, and I gently laid her on the ground near Demris's cave.

What happened? Sion asked, eyeing Maren's prone form with concern.

I think she pushed herself too far. She passed out after casting her last spell.

You're bleeding. Are you all right?

I glanced down at my arm. The pain remained, but the bleeding was starting to subside. *I'm fine. Is Bryngar still here in the stable?*

No. He left after feeding us. Did you lift his curse?

We returned the amulet, so he should look normal again. Watch over Maren. I'm going to find him.

I pressed my injured arm close to my body and left the warmth of the cave. Darkness enveloped the landscape. We'd been in the tomb longer than I thought. The wind and cold didn't seem as intense, though the trudge through the deep snow was still an arduous task. I marched to the school, suddenly heavy with exhaustion.

The door swung open easily when I pushed on it, and I slipped inside just as an unfamiliar figure was coming out of the throne room.

"Bryngar?"

"I am glad to see you have returned," he said, beaming.

As he stepped into the light, I saw that other than his size, he looked nothing like his father. His shoulders were broad and well-defined, and his muscular arms bore countless scars. Framed by a thick mane of blond hair, his face was weathered from the harsh temperatures, and his piercing blue eyes gleamed with fortitude. A bushy, reddish-blond beard reached down to the middle of his chest.

"I see the curse is broken. Returning the amulet worked just as you said."

"Yes. I felt the magic fade and looked in the mirror to see I was myself again. I am grateful for your help." He looked past me. "Where is Maren?"

"She's in the stable. The wards in the tomb drained her, and she fell unconscious after we killed a creature that was guarding the tomb."

"So it is true," Bryngar said. "The legends tell of a guardian who watches over the *volur*. I must confess, I did not believe it was real."

"It was real," I replied, showing him the gash on my arm. "I was lucky to escape with my life."

"I am indebted to you, to both of you. I will do as I promised and rally my people. Come, let us bring Maren in here to rest. I will leave to seek my brethren, but you are welcome to stay as long as you need to."

"I appreciate your hospitality. Hopefully, Maren will wake up soon. We are pressed for time already."

We returned to the stable, and Bryngar insisted on carrying Maren.

"Do not stress your wound," he said. "It is the least I can do."

She was tiny compared to his bulk, and he cradled her in his arms as though she were an infant. We trekked back to the school, and Bryngar led us up the stairs to the second floor. The room he gave us seemed familiar, and I assumed it was the same room we stayed in the first time we visited Valgaard. He placed Maren on the enormous bed and spread a thick blanket over her to keep her warm.

"I will bring you some bandages for your arm. You can clean the wound in the bathing chamber down the hall."

"Thank you," I replied.

Bryngar left the room, and I sat on the edge of the bed and stared at Maren, watching the gentle rise and fall of her chest as she breathed. I checked her pulse again, and it was noticeably stronger than before. I was trying not to worry about her, but I was reminded of the time she fell unconscious while battling the griffon riders of Midia.

Midia.

Maren wanted to seek their aid as well. Now that we'd gained the support of Valgaard, I knew she would want to go to Midia next. That journey could be more dangerous than battling the creature in the tomb, but we needed all the help we could get. I was deep in thought when Bryngar returned, and his appearance startled me.

"You need to tend to your wound," he said firmly, eyeing me critically. "Are you feeling well?"

"I'm fine. Just thinking." I stood and accepted the bandages from him. "Thank you. As much as I don't want to spend the night here, I think it will be necessary for Maren's sake."

"I know you are in a hurry, but healing cannot be rushed, especially the kind she needs. Stay here and rest. She will not be helpful to anyone otherwise. Do you need anything before I leave?"

"You're going to travel through this weather in the dark?" I asked.

Bryngar chuckled. "I am used to it. This is my domain, after all. I will be fine. Once I have gathered my people, we will meet you at the Citadel."

"Thank you again. For everything. Other than food, I think we are fine."

"I have already prepared two packs with rations for you. You can find them on the table in the throne room."

"You are the king, yet you treat us like royalty. It is a welcome change."

Bryngar scowled. "King? I am king in name only. No," he shook his head. "I am no king, only a rider like yourself. The foolish pride of Valgaard will die. I will see to that."

I had my doubts about his intentions, but not anymore. He clapped a hand on my shoulder and grinned. "Safe travels, my friend."

"And to you, as well," I replied.

After he left, I went to the bathing chamber and washed and dressed my arm, then returned to the room and climbed into the bed next to Maren. I wanted to stay awake and watch over her, but I knew that wasn't wise. I needed my own rest. Morning would come quickly, and there was no telling what awaited us.

10

When I awoke, shafts of pale light shone through the windows. I blinked a few times and rubbed my eyes, then looked over at Maren. She was awake, her head resting against her left arm as she stared at me.

"How are you feeling?" I asked.

"Refreshed," she replied with a grin. "What about you?"

I lifted my bandaged arm and flexed the muscles, relieved to find the pain had dulled to a mere ache. "It's better."

Maren frowned. "What happened to your arm?"

"That creature from the tomb stepped on me. It left a gash, but it wasn't anything serious."

"Did we kill it? My memory is a little fuzzy."

"Yes. You brought the ceiling down on it, and there was enough blood to ensure it was dead. You passed out after that."

"And you carried me here?" she asked.

"Not quite." I relayed the details of Bryngar insisting he bring her from the stable and everything else she missed while she was unconscious.

"I wish I could have thanked him before he left. It sounds like he truly did learn from his father's mistakes."

"I'm convinced," I said. "I wasn't at first, but I am now."

Maren stretched and cuddled up close to me, nuzzling her face against my neck. "It would be nice to relax for once."

"Once this is all over, we'll make time to relax."

"Promise?"

"Of course."

"Good. I guess we should get moving. The quicker we get to Midia, the quicker we can go home."

"True." I kissed Maren on the forehead before untangling myself from her embrace. "We should eat something first. Bryngar prepared some rations for us."

Maren agreed, and together we made our way downstairs to the throne room. We sat at the table and ate a small meal from the food in the packs. A cursory glance inside them revealed bread, cheeses, some fruit, and some sort of meat. It was enough to get us to our next destination.

After we finished eating, we went to the stable and mounted up. The wind gusts weren't as fierce as the previous night, but the cold air still felt like it was freezing my bones.

We are almost gone from this place, Sion said, listening to my thoughts.

I know. Try to take us down the mountain quickly if you can. I'm ready for the sun to warm my skin.

Sion stepped out of the cave, and I braced against the biting cold, trying vainly to shrink into my cloak. She took to the air, gaining altitude before turning east. I crouched low in the saddle and pressed my face into my arm, seeking shelter from the cold until we were out of its reach.

We flew for a few hours before landing near a densely wooded area. It was good to leave the harsh terrain of Valgaard behind. I dismounted and walked among the trees, stretching my legs. Maren joined me, and the sound of rustling leaves and the distant chirping of birds filled the air as we wandered deeper into the forest. The serenity of nature was a stark contrast to the events of the last day.

The dense canopy above created a natural shelter, and I marveled at the vibrant colors that surrounded us, from the lush greens of the trees to the delicate wildflowers that dotted the forest floor. Maren reached down and plucked a small blossom, twirling it between her fingers. Her smile was enchanting, lighting up her face like a radiant sunrise.

"Do you think I'm crazy for wanting to go to Midia?" she asked.

"Crazy? No." I shook my head. "Odd? Maybe a little." I laughed as she playfully punched me in the arm.

"I'm serious."

She sighed, her fingers releasing the delicate flower she held. It spun in circles until it landed on the ground. "It's just... I want to do what is right for Osnen and for the Order, and I know that stopping my uncle *is* the right thing, but I also fear the unknown. Valgaard was a risk, sure, but we had an idea of what we were dealing with. Not so much with Midia."

"I understand," I said. "The Order is already weak. If Shadamar falls, will the nobles squabble for power, causing more problems? We don't have the numbers to keep things from spiraling into chaos. On the other hand, what if Midia decides to invade? Neither situation would be ideal, but all we can do is hope for the best and plan for the worst."

We stood in silence, the uncertainty of the future hanging heavily over both of us.

"There's also the issue of the dragon slayers," I added. "I'm sure Bryngar will do what he can to dissuade them, but we cannot disregard the idea that we may be facing a war on two fronts while the nobles divide us from within."

You both make things sound hopeless, Sion said. *As long as you are breathing, there is hope.*

Do you not have any worries?

Dragons worry about few things, but even then, we do not let those thoughts consume us.

That's easier said than done.

You must take your thoughts captive. Bend them to your will. The future is unpredictable, but your actions today have the power to shape it. What you do today can influence what tomorrow brings.

I mentally digested her words, and they brought me a measure of comfort.

You are wiser than me, I admitted.

Of course I am. I'm a dragon. She chortled, her laughter echoing into the bond.

I shook my head, a grin on my face.

"What?" Maren asked, her expression lifting with her own smile.

"Sion. She fancies herself a comedian sometimes."

"I'm constantly fascinated by the varying personalities of dragons. Sion has a great sense of humor, while Demris is much more focused and serious."

"They are unique, just like us. I think it's easy to forget that." I paused and took her hand in mine, pulling her close. "If you think there's a chance going to Midia will help, then I say we should go. You have trusted me with every decision I have made, regardless of the outcome. I will gladly do the same for you."

Maren smiled and hugged me tightly. "It looks like we're going to Midia, then."

THE FLIGHT TO THE BORDER was uneventful. No royal riders were prowling the skies, and the wind was blowing in our favor, so we made excellent time. We crossed into Midia and as we flew over the valley where we fought the dracolich, a contingent of griffon riders swarmed up to meet us.

Sion growled menacingly, and they kept a safe distance except for the leader. He drew close and motioned for us to follow him. I nodded in acknowledgment, and he took up a position in front of us.

They led us north and Araphel came into view. Constructed on top of an extinct volcano, the castle was surrounded by an extensive network of structures that served as the headquarters for the kingdom's military. Immense catapults and ballista were carefully arranged in rows outside the protective walls. I had assumed the castle would be abandoned after the war, but it was very much still in use.

It looks the same as the day we saw it last, Sion said.

I know. It feels weird coming back here. This is where we first learned to strengthen our bond, but it's also where my father's risen corpse was enslaved.

The tangle of emotions was a complicated web. As we landed in the courtyard, the griffon riders dispersed, leaving Maren and me alone amid soldiers bustling about their duties. Anticipation laced the air as news of our arrival spread like wildfire. Maren and I dismounted, and I glanced around uneasily, unsure if Sion and Demris would be safe among the enemy.

Do not worry about me. I will flame them all to ash before they get close enough to attack.

I patted Sion on the shoulder, and a man about my age strode over and looked us up and down. His face revealed nothing, but I had the feeling he wasn't happy with our presence.

"Since you came here peacefully, I will extend grace. What brings you to Araphel?" he asked.

I cleared my throat. "We are here as emissaries from the Citadel in Osnen. We seek an audience with your king."

The man made a noise in his throat. "Emissaries? How do I know you aren't assassins come to kill our leader?"

"You don't," Maren replied. "You'll just have to trust us. As you said, we came peacefully."

We stood in silence for a moment, and the man nodded. "Very well. Follow me."

Whispers followed us as we made our way toward the castle entrance. Inside, the familiar corridors resonated with echoes from the past. The stone walls seemed to hold the weight of countless memories, both joyous and painful. I couldn't help but feel a sense of unease creeping up my spine, a silent reminder of the battle fought within these very halls. Before he turned traitor, this was where Hrodin had killed the False King.

"Wait here," the man said, leaving us in an antechamber surrounded by armed guards. I glanced at Maren. She returned my gaze, but neither of us said anything. The minutes ticked by, and finally, the soldier returned.

"His Majesty has agreed to see you. This way."

We followed him down a long corridor, passing by portraits and tapestries that hung on the walls. The corridor ended at two thick wooden doors, which several guards pushed open as we approached.

The throne room was dimly lit. A single orb of light illuminated the center of the chamber, where a tall figure sat on the throne.

Statues lined the carpet that led to the oversized chair, and spaced between them were soldiers standing at attention.

Our escort waved us ahead, and Maren and I walked side by side down the carpet. When we reached the end of the rug, we stopped and knelt in unison.

"When I received word that dragons had flown across the border, I expected to see an army at our doorstep. Instead, I see…" The king paused. "Eldwin? Is that you?"

I slowly raised my head to look at him. A face framed with a neatly trimmed white beard stared back at me. His short hair matched the color of his facial hair, and his light green eyes sparked a faint sense of familiarity. Time seemed to rewind, and my eyes widened in recognition.

"Altin?"

"You'll address the king as Your Highness," the man behind me gruffly said.

"Peace, Taran," Altin commanded. "Eldwin is a friend of mine. He is exempt from formalities." His gaze shifted to Maren. "And any friend of Eldwin is more than welcome. Rise."

Altin stepped down from the throne and came to wrap me in a hug as I stood. I returned the embrace, and he stepped back, taking in my appearance.

"I am glad to see you are still alive. How is your dragon?"

"She's good," I replied. "She is here if you want to see her."

"I would like that. Who is your friend?"

"This is my wife, Maren. Maren Toft."

Altin's brows rose in surprise as he looked at her with renewed interest. "The daughter of Erling Toft?"

"The same," Maren replied. "It is a pleasure to meet you. Eldwin told me much about his time here with you and…" she glanced at me. "And his father."

"Yes, those were troubling times. I am sad to say that I believed Dagnis's lies for too long. But those days are behind us now."

"You're the king of Midia now? I thought you fled the kingdom?" I asked.

"I did," Altin said. "Once I heard that Dagnis and his necromancer had been defeated, I came back. This place is my home, after all. I wanted to return to my shop, but the people were adamant that I take over as king. I didn't feel worthy of the title. After all I had been complicit with, I didn't think I was fit to lead anyone."

"And yet here you are."

"Here I am. The people spoke, and who am I to refuse them of what they want?"

"I am sure you are a good king," I said. "Your heart was always in the right place, even if your loyalty wasn't. The False King deceived many, not just you."

"Let us change the direction of our conversation. I do not like to dwell on the past, especially *that* part. What brings you to Midia?"

"Do you remember what you wanted from me and my dragon when we first met?"

"Yes, of course. I wanted your help."

"With what, exactly?"

"With saving my kingdom."

I nodded. "Now it is I who asks the same of you."

"What do you mean?"

"I'm not a fool of the ways of the world," Maren chimed in. "I'm sure you have spies in Osnen. Have you not heard what is happening?"

Altin shifted uncomfortably. "I've heard some rumors, but it's been difficult to distinguish the truth."

"My father decided he no longer wanted anyone to challenge his authority. He tried to destroy the Order. He's dead now, but his brother has taken the throne and seeks to finish what my father started."

"So Erling *is* dead. I heard he was assassinated."

"Not quite," I said. "He was injured, and I ended his suffering."

I expected Altin to be horrified, but he merely nodded. "Erling's ego is no surprise to me, though it is odd he wanted to destroy the Order. From what I understand, the riders have always heeded his commands. Did that change?"

"No," Maren replied. "I have my suspicions that my father was plotting something, and he was concerned that the Order would interfere with his plans."

"I see. And now your uncle wants to destroy the Order as well? That is troubling. Whatever this plot is, it cannot be good." Altin looked from Maren to me. "I am hesitant to offer my help. Crossing the border with an army would be seen as an act of war, and that would only make matters worse."

"I understand your hesitation too well, as I'm sure you remember," I said.

Altin sighed and rubbed a hand over his beard. "Indeed, I do remember," he murmured. "I cannot turn a blind eye to those in need, and I would not see another Dagnis in power, in Midia *or* Osnen. Let me consider what you've said. In the meantime, I will hold a feast in your honor. Taran, please give them lodging, then organize the preparations."

"As you wish, Your Majesty."

Altin drew close and lowered his voice. "I will do what I can to help you, but I do not yet know what that will look like. Get some rest, and I will see you both shortly."

"What about our dragons?" Maren asked.

"They will be well taken care of."

"It is good to see you again, Altin," I said.

He smiled, but there was a hint of sadness in his eyes.

12

TARAN LED US OUT OF the throne room and down the myriad of corridors to an empty guest room. The furnishings were opulent compared to those at the Citadel, but there was nothing comfortable about them. While Altin was friendly and welcoming, we were among enemies. Once we were alone, I sat on a wooden bench beside the window and stared out at the battlements.

"I think we're wasting our time here," I said. "We should head back to Osnen."

"Altin said he would consider our request. Waiting is the hardest part of any endeavor."

"The look in his eyes tells me he isn't going to help us. Not in any meaningful way."

Maren joined me on the bench and stroked her fingers through my hair. "You know him better than I do. If he won't help, then so be it. At least we tried."

A few hours later, Maren and I were summoned to join the festivities. We entered the grand hall, and the sounds of music and laughter filled the air. A dozen or more tables were lined up in the shape of an enormous rectangle, and Altin was at the head of one end. He motioned for us to join him, and after we sat down, he stood and raised his goblet. A hush fell over the room.

"Tonight, we gather not only to celebrate peace, but also to honor Eldwin and Maren. They are friends of mine, and therefore friends of Midia. We have overcome dark times, and now we enjoy the fruits of those labors."

The room erupted in cheers and applause as Altin raised his goblet to toast. The metallic rings of people clashing their cups together echoed throughout the room. The feast was a lavish affair, with delicacies from all corners of the kingdom laid out. Maren and I ate and drank, though I was careful not to consume too much of the mead that was being served.

A troupe of performers acted out a play that depicted the triumph over the False King. It was a humorous and lively performance, filled with exaggerated gestures and comical dialogue. The audience roared with laughter at the antics of the actors, their spirits lifted by the joyous celebration.

As I watched the play unfold, I couldn't help but notice Altin's eyes occasionally flicker toward me. There was a thoughtfulness in his gaze, and I wondered what he was considering, what decision he would make.

When the play came to an end and the performers took their final bow, Altin stood once more, holding his goblet high. The room fell silent again, anticipation hanging heavy in the air.

"I must step away for a moment, but please, continue to enjoy the food and entertainment."

Altin nodded at me, and I rose to my feet. Maren quickly wiped her mouth on a cloth, and the three of us departed, escorted by a contingent of guards. We left the great hall and went to a small chamber near the throne room.

"What's going on?" I asked, suddenly nervous. Altin's demeanor hadn't changed, but taking us to a secluded room was odd.

"Leave us," Altin told the guards. They hesitated to obey, and he waved his hands at them. "Go. I'm in no danger with them, and I will leave the door unlatched."

The guards begrudgingly exited the chamber.

"I do not want prying ears to listen to our conversation. Although I consider you my friends, there are still people in Midia who hold a grudge against Osnen because of Dagnis's lies. With time, those feelings will fade."

"Have you made a decision?" Maren asked.

"Straight to the point." Altin chuckled. His expression turned serious, and he spoke his next words slowly. "I'm sorry, but I'm afraid I cannot assist you."

His words didn't surprise me. Our kingdoms were sworn enemies, and it was a daunting request to ask someone to take on such a risk without any personal gain.

Maren's jaw tightened. "Why not?"

"My people finally have peace. That is not something I am willing to take away."

"Did you ask them if they wanted to aid us? After all, you said yourself you don't speak for them."

"You twist my words," Altin said. "Put yourself in my position. Would you really lead your army to certain destruction?"

"Nothing is certain," I replied. "With our riders and Valgaard's, we have a formidable force. Your strength will ensure we win."

"You don't understand how dangerous Shadamar is, do you?"

"Maren is of the same bloodline. If you are worried about his magic, we have sorcerers of our own. The Citadel currently stands because of them. Magic does not give him an advantage."

"You haven't seen half of what he can do."

"And you have?" Maren asked.

"Yes."

That gave me pause. "I don't understand. You've been to Osnen?"

"No, of course not. Shadamar is cut from the same cloth as the Necromancer. Most people do not delve into dark magic by their own choice. They are drawn into it, seduced to its power by another."

"Are you saying Shadamar studied magic under the Necromancer?" I asked.

"They were both students under the same master. If I aid you, I become a target, as do my people. I do not want Midia to see any more suffering than it already has."

"So you're afraid," Maren said, crossing her arms.

"Afraid?" Altin scoffed. "No, afraid doesn't come close. I'm terrified. If you could see what I have, you would be, too. Whatever spells are protecting the Citadel can't stop Shadamar. The only reason he hasn't broken through them yet is because he's chosen not to."

A sense of dread gnawed at my insides as he spoke, and I couldn't shake the feeling that he was telling us the truth. If Shadamar was as powerful as he was sly, and I had no doubts that he was, then it would make sense he was hiding his true prowess.

"If you won't send your army, at least tell us how to defeat him."

"The only thing I know is that you cannot kill him with magic. Not unless you explore the dark arts yourself, and I do not recommend that."

Maren frowned. "Is there anything you *can* do?"

Despite no one else being present, Altin lowered his voice. "I know a group of mercenaries who will take on any job for the right price. I've hired them in the past to complete some tasks for me. They may be small in numbers, but each member is worth at least ten regular soldiers. They might just be crazy enough to go up against your uncle."

"We'll take any help we can get," I said. "But unfortunately, we don't have that kind of gold."

"Don't worry about the money. I'll take care of it."

"Thank you. I—we," I glanced at Maren, "appreciate it."

"I wish I could do more, but I can't risk it. I hope you understand."

"I don't like it, but I get it," Maren said.

"Where can we find these mercenaries?"

"You can't. I'll send them a message. If they are interested in taking the job, they'll come to the Citadel. I think they'll be apt to help you. Their leader is a former rider, after all."

13

ALTHOUGH IT WAS LATE IN the afternoon, Maren and I decided it was best to return home. We had done all we could, and now it was time to prepare for the inevitable. Sion and Demris flew side by side, and I kept a vigilant watch despite there being nothing to see. The wind whipped through my hair, carrying with it whispers of uncertainty and fear.

The impending battle loomed over me like a storm cloud. I stared at Maren for a long moment, wondering what I had done to be blessed with her. She wasn't perfect. Far from it, but she was perfect for me. She saw past my flaws, both visible and invisible, and loved me despite them.

Maren noticed I was staring and looked at me questioningly. I shook my head slightly to let her know nothing was wrong and turned my gaze ahead.

Do you think Valgaard will be enough? I asked Sion. *If Altin sent his army, I know we could defeat Shadamar. Without their help, I'm not so sure we can.*

We have seen hardships before, some more difficult than this. As long as the Order stays united, we will triumph.

Your confidence gives me hope. We flew in silence, and my thoughts turned to the mercenaries Altin had mentioned.

Do you remember when we first found each other?

How could I forget? Sion replied.

You were being taken to someone who had bought you, a mercenary leader. Her name was Seren. She was a former member of the Order until her dragon died. I wonder if Altin was talking about her group.

That seems likely. If she was a rider, I am sure she will come to help us.

Yes, I think she will. I remember she was rather imposing, but she was nice to me. She knew my father, too. None of that means she will come, though.

All we can do is wait and see.

As we reached the outskirts of the Citadel, a sense of melancholy settled over me. The familiar sights that once brought comfort now seemed tinged with sadness. The rolling hills and lush forests, which had always been a testament to our land's beauty and prosperity, now served as a stark reminder of what was at stake.

There was no sign of Shadamar or his army, and a portion of the barrier opened to allow Sion and Demris inside. We landed in the courtyard and were immediately greeted by Katori and Henrik.

"What news?" Henrik asked.

"Valgaard is coming." I didn't see the point in mentioning our trip to Midia since that had been disappointing. "Shadamar may be here by the time they arrive, but it's better they are late than to not come at all. Any luck on finding supplies?"

"Yes, and there is more good news. We found Master Anesko. He's in rough shape, but he's alive."

"Thank the gods," I said. "Where was he?"

"North of Branshire. The party was ambushed by Shadamar's men, and all but Anesko fell in battle. His dragon managed to get them somewhere safe to hide, but he's worse off than Anesko. They'll survive, but they won't be able to do much while they heal."

Our numbers continue to dwindle, I told Sion.

We will rise from the ashes stronger than before.

I wasn't so sure of that, but I kept my thoughts away from the bond.

"At least they are safe now," Maren said. "How are the preparations going?"

Henrik deferred to Katori.

"We have done all we can," she answered. "Today is the last day of mourning, and our scouts say the king's army is preparing to march. They should be here within two days. When should we expect the riders from Valgaard to arrive?"

"Hopefully before then," I replied. "The school was abandoned except for Bryngar. He was under a curse, but Maren and I helped break it, and he went to find his people after it was lifted."

Katori tilted her head to the side. "Who is Bryngar?"

"Hrodin's son."

"Can he be trusted?" Henrik asked.

"I believe so. He treated us well and seemed sincere when he told us he wanted to regain their honor. They will come. I'm sure of it."

"I hope you're right."

I could sense the doubt in Henrik's voice, but I didn't blame him. Our situation was dire, and putting our trust in those who betrayed us was a risky move, but trusting anyone these days carried its own set of risks.

Sion and Demris retreated below ground to the stables, and Maren and I went to see Anesko. He was asleep, so we left him to rest and quietly exited the infirmary. The rest of the day passed slowly, uncertainty lingering in the air like a heavy fog. As we walked through the Citadel's corridors, I couldn't help but notice the tension etched across the faces of the other riders.

After dinner, we gathered with the other Curates and discussed our battle strategy repeatedly. Each time we went through it, doubts would creep in and force me to question if we were truly prepared for what was to come.

Tired of talking in circles, Maren and I retired to our quarters, seeking solace in each other's presence. I could hear the distant sounds of soldiers marching along the parapets, the clanking of armor drifting through the window. It was a haunting symphony. Wrapped in each other's embrace, we whispered our fears into the darkness and eventually found peace in sleep.

As the days passed, anticipation hung heavy in the air. Everyone knew that defeating Shadamar would not be easy, but no one gave in to despair. The Assembly joined our discussions, offering their insights and unwavering support.

On the evening of the third day, as the sun dipped below the horizon and cast a fiery glow across the land, a messenger arrived. He carried a sealed scroll with Altin's emblem pressed into the wax—news that the mercenaries were on their way. He also delivered the news that Shadamar's forces were closing in and would soon arrive at the gates.

As the night grew deeper, I found myself restless and unable to sleep, my mind consumed with thoughts of what lay ahead. The looming battle weighed heavily on my heart, for I knew lives would be lost, and sacrifices made. But there was no turning back. We had to stand and fight because that was the only option aside from death.

A horn blared outside, jolting me awake. The first rays of dawn slanted through the window. Morning had come, and with it, the impending threat of war.

14

As Maren and I stood on the ramparts and looked out over the sprawling camp of Shadamar's army, the Citadel bustled with activity behind us. Riders scurried about, finalizing the defenses and preparing for the coming battle. Katori and Henrik, along with the other Curates, were present, overseeing the preparations.

"Any word from Valgaard?" I asked.

"Nothing yet," Maren replied.

Drums beat, and I watched the enemy lines swell, slowly gathering into orderly formations.

"What are they doing? The barrier is impenetrable. Why are they mobilizing?"

Maren's face was serious as she turned to me. "Shadamar is always scheming. The real question is, what exactly is he plotting?"

I thought about what Altin had told us about Shadamar's magic. *You haven't seen half of what he can do.* Lifting my gaze, I studied the barrier. A sense of dread washed over me.

"He's going to destroy it," I said.

"He can't."

"Can't he? How much magical energy does it take the sorcerers to keep it up?"

"A lot," Maren replied. "But they work in shifts to keep their strength up."

"What happens when the barrier gets struck? Does it take more effort to keep it in place?"

The expression on Maren's face told me she understood what I was hinting at. "Yes, but…" She looked at Shadamar's forces. The royal riders took to the air, casting long shadows over the ground forces as they wheeled overhead.

"I think you're right, but if the barrier falls—"

"Then we need to be ready," I said. "Let's just hope that doesn't happen before Bryngar and his riders get here."

"We can't assume they'll be here in time."

"I'll warn the others."

I descended the ramparts in search of Katori and found her with Henrik. "What's the plan if the barrier falls?"

"We take to the sky and engage the enemy from above," Henrik answered. "We've already considered that possibility."

"It's not a possibility, it's going to happen. And I think Shadamar intends to bring it down quickly."

As if to prove my words, a thunderous crack split the air as ballista bolts shattered against the barrier.

"Everyone needs to be ready. Does Master Anesko know Shadamar is here?"

"Yes, he does," Katori said. "He tried to leave his bed, but I told him to stay there and rest. He is not in any shape to fight."

I knew he probably wasn't, but if the protection of the barrier disappeared, we would need every rider we had, regardless of injuries. Saying that would sound heartless, so I kept those words to myself.

"If there's a consistent barrage, how long do we have before the shield drops?"

"Half a day," Katori answered. "Maybe longer. It is hard to say."

"That doesn't give us much time, but it's better than nothing."

We stared at one another in silence before Henrik said, "If anything happens, it's been an honor knowing you both."

Katori bowed her head.

"The only thing that's going to happen today is the death of another king." My words were heartfelt, but I knew the likelihood of us winning was almost nonexistent.

We parted ways, and I headed for the stable. Sion was in her cave. In the dim light, her eyes shone like a feline's, and her sharp claws scraped against the hard stone as she exited, her tail twitching restlessly behind her.

Is it time?

Not yet, I replied. *It won't be long, though. The battle will probably unfold in the streets.*

Sion growled, the sound sending vibrations through the stone beneath my feet. For a brief moment, I entertained the thought of fleeing. It was foolish. Where would we go? Shadamar would pursue us wherever we went. And besides that, Maren would never leave. Not willingly, anyway.

We will not run, Sion said firmly, sensing my wayward feelings through the bond. *It is time to fight for what remains.*

I know. Ignore those thoughts. They are born from fear.

There is nothing wrong with being afraid, but you must not let your fear dictate your actions. Remember what I said. You must bend your thoughts to your will.

Yes, I remember. I'll try harder.

That is all I can ask of you.

I just came down here to let you know.

We both knew I could have told her without coming to the stable, but standing in her presence gave me strength and made me feel braver than I was. She lowered her head and pressed her snout to my forehead. I rested my hands on the sides of her face and closed my eyes, basking in the moment.

As the warmth of Sion's touch enveloped me, a sense of calm washed over my troubled mind. In that simple gesture, I found solace and reassurance. Sion understood the magnitude of the task ahead, and her unwavering support only bolstered my resolve.

With newfound determination, I left the stable and made my way back to the ramparts. Maren was still there, and we stood quietly, watching as the bombardment of catapults, ballista, and magical attacks pummeled the shield. It was holding steady for now, but the strain was evident in the flickering pulses of light that emanated from its surface. The air crackled and hummed with energy, and I wasn't so sure that Katori's estimate was correct.

"We need to do something," Maren whispered.

"What can we do? We're stuck here. If we leave the Citadel, he'll follow us. This is where we make our last stand."

Maren turned to look at me. "Exactly! This is where it ends. If I know my uncle, he thinks we'll wait until the barrier falls to fight. What if we surprise him?"

"Surprise him how? We're outnumbered."

"I don't know if it's possible, but I just had an idea. We could reverse the barrier."

"What do you mean reverse it?"

"Instead of keeping it around the Citadel, we can place it over the camp. It will seal them inside."

"How does that help us?" I asked. "It'll just protect them."

"They won't be able to leave it, which effectively traps them inside. And then we can shrink it."

"If it shrinks, it'll—" My eyes widened in realization. "You're brilliant!"

"I know." Maren smiled. "But in order to reverse it, we'll have to drop it first. That will leave a brief window of time where we aren't protected."

"It's worth the risk. And if we fall, we will fall together."

15

While Maren aided the sorcerers with the new plan, I was in the courtyard with the other riders, mounted and ready for anything unexpected. I absent-mindedly rubbed Sion's neck scales while my eyes remained on the barrier.

Projectiles relentlessly pummeled the barrier, targeting a specific portion. We evacuated everyone from the area behind that focal point, anticipating significant destruction once the barrier faded.

On top of the ballista bolts and magical attacks, the royal riders occasionally flew overhead, their dragons breathing their flames onto the shield. It flickered with every strike. At first, I thought it was a sign of its impending failure, but it became evident it was merely a visible display of the strain on those keeping it up.

We should be prepared to fight the king's men if the barrier falls while they fly overhead, Sion said.

Maren said they will drop the barrier when there's a lull.

I felt Sion's muscles tense under me. *I can feel the magic receding. Get ready!*

The seconds ticked by and there was no change. Slowly, sections of the barrier rippled and became wispy like dye poured into water before dissipating from view. Several ballista bolts flew over the walls and crashed into the ground. A moment later, a bolt of lightning zig-zagged across the sky and struck the western side of the Citadel, scattering broken pieces of stone.

A cheer rang out.

They think they destroyed the shield, I said.

We could use that to our advantage. Come on!

Sion leaped into the air. I gripped the reins tightly as she ascended, her powerful wings beating against the air.

What are you doing?

Drawing their attention, she replied. *If they focus on us, they won't breach the Citadel.*

A chorus of roars filled the air as the other riders took to the sky behind us. We soared over the wall, the wind whipping through my hair. Below us, chaos ensued. Thinking they had broken through the barrier, Shadamar's men charged forward without hesitation. There were so many of them. They streamed across the land like a tidal wave, their armor flashing under the morning sun.

Sion unleashed a fiery breath that engulfed a group of soldiers pushing a battering ram toward the main gates. They screamed, and I scrunched my nose in disgust as the stench of burning flesh hit my nostrils. An arrow whizzed through the air near my head, and Sion banked sharply to the left, smashing her tail into the center of a siege tower. The wood splintered and men cried out as the upper portion fell, crushing them as it collapsed to the ground.

We darted over the battlefield, Sion's fire and claws tearing through the enemy ranks. The other riders followed our lead, descending like a storm and ravaging everything in their path. Chaos settled over the battlefield as the soldiers, realizing the ruse, began scrambling to retreat.

I admired the ferocity of our attack, and the element of surprise had given us an advantage, allowing us to strike fear into their hearts, but I knew it wouldn't last. We were outnumbered, and the royal riders were circling to engage us.

Get back to the Citadel, I said. *The tides are about to turn against us.*

Sion ignored me, her lust for battle in control. The bond flooded with her rage, and she breathed a long torrent of flames, sweeping her head left and right. The cries of the wounded and dying drifted up to us. Instead of trying to push through her fury, I scanned the battlefield looking for Shadamar.

A horn blared, and I glanced over my shoulder. Behind the school, an immense mass of clouds quickly approached.

What is that? I asked, but Sion was deaf to my question.

It grew closer, and I smiled as soon as I realized it wasn't clouds. It was an army of white dragons. Bryngar had rallied his people. Valgaard had come!

My fist shot up as I let out a battle cry. Sion joined me, matching my roar, and the white dragons echoed our cries with a deafening boom that seemed to shake the very air.

We can do this, I thought. *We can end this here and now.*

Yes, we can, Sion growled, reading my mind. *There's the king!*

I turned my attention ahead and saw him. He rode a black horse, and a contingent of mounted soldiers in plate armor surrounded him.

Why isn't the barrier up yet? It's taking too long. Something must be wrong.

I can sense something. It's subtle, but I think it's blocking the spell from forming.

It's coming from Shadamar, isn't it?

There was a pause before she answered. *Yes.*

Take me to him.

I could feel Sion's hesitation in the bond. *He won't let us get that close.*

She was probably right, but I knew that wasn't why she said it. She feared for my safety. I did, too. If he were an ordinary man, I would have no issue defeating him in fair combat, but Shadamar was anything but ordinary.

Take me, I repeated.

Sion rumbled her objection, but she veered toward his position. As we got closer, the battle intensified. The white dragons clashed with the royal riders, their roars and screeches filling the air. Flames and ice swirled above our heads, casting a ghostly glow onto the battlefield. Sion propelled us forward with incredible speed, dodging arrows and spears.

She dove, her massive wings tucked in as we descended. The ground rushed up to meet us, and I braced myself for impact. Sion's talons touched down, raking furrows into the dirt, and I leaped off her back and drew my sword in one fluid motion. Sion towered behind me, snapping her jaws menacingly.

"Surrender," I shouted. "Surrender or die!"

16

"You've brought friends," Shadamar said with a sneer. "It won't matter. The Order will die today."

He dismounted from his horse and ordered his guards to stand aside. A surge of adrenaline coursed through my veins. This was it—my chance to end this war. Sion let out a thunderous roar that echoed across the battlefield. I lifted my sword and took a defensive stance, but I knew Shadamar was unlikely to give me a fair fight.

Tell me if you sense he's using magic, I told Sion. *I can't defend against it, but maybe I can draw his focus enough that Maren and the others can get the barrier back up.*

I will.

"Why do you want to destroy the Order? It's been around for centuries and has always aided the crown."

"Aided the crown?" Shadamar laughed. "That means nothing to me. The Order has grown weak. It is a hindrance to progress, and without new dragons, the Order will die off. Better to end it quickly now than to watch it suffer and fade slowly. Your dragons are nothing more than glorified pets."

I am no pet, Sion growled.

Shadamar wagged a finger at her. "Don't do anything foolish."

"You're lucky she hasn't flamed you yet," I said.

"Let her try. Her flames cannot harm me."

Don't humor him. Let's just keep him busy.

"You bore me. I don't understand what my niece sees in you. You're crippled, a low born, and have nothing to offer her. Like the rest of the Order, you are a leach on society."

I'd heard worse insults growing up as a child. "If you surrender now, we'll let you live out the rest of your days in the dungeon. Otherwise, I'm afraid you won't be leaving here alive."

"Don't play with me, boy. I could snuff the life from you with a snap of my fingers."

"Fight me like a man," I taunted. "No magic. Just steel and skill."

Without warning, Shadamar lunged forward, his movements swift and calculated. His sword flashed from its scabbard faster than I thought possible, but I managed to parry his first strike, our blades clashing with a resounding clang that reverberated through the air.

Sion's protective instincts kicked in, and she sprang past me, her maw coming within inches of Shadamar's head before she came to a sudden stop.

"No dragons, either," Shadamar said. He flicked his wrist and Sion was thrown aside by an invisible force. She tried to get up, but something kept her pinned down.

"Don't touch her," I said through clenched teeth.

"I'm only leveling the field."

I attacked, and Shadamar parried my thrusts effortlessly. His movements were graceful and fluid, leaving me struggling to keep up. We continued to exchange blows, the clang of each one ringing loudly in my ears. Sion remained pinned to the ground, but her presence was an unwavering source of strength.

He's toying with me, I told Sion. *He's faster and stronger than I am.*

It's subtle, but he's enhancing his movements with magic.

I wish I could do the same.

Pull what you need from the bond to keep your strength up. I can feel the exhaustion rising in you.

I drew on Sion's strength and immediately felt my energy return. Breaking away from Shadamar, I wiped the sweat from my brow. "You're using magic. I thought maybe you had more honor than Erling, but obviously not."

My words must have struck a nerve because Shadamar's face twisted in anger, and he snarled. The air hummed, causing the hairs on my arms to stand on end. Tendrils of black shadows flew out from him and struck me, sending me reeling backward. I crashed into Sion's immobile body, but quickly regained my footing. The tendrils retreated and faded from view.

What was that?

It was dark magic, Sion replied. *You should flee.*

I'm not leaving you here. We still need to draw his focus away from blocking the barrier spell.

He will kill you. You need to run.

Shadamar's guards looked up and began shouting. He ignored them, and they turned their mounts around and spurred them into a gallop. I glanced at the sky and saw the reason for their hasty retreat. A white dragon had been killed and his body was falling straight toward our position.

With no hesitation, Shadamar uttered a few words and conjured a cone of vibrant red energy from his right hand. The powerful beam shot through the sky with incredible speed before colliding with the fallen dragon, sending it careening off course. With a deafening crash, the creature tumbled to the ground a short distance away, creating a cloud of dust and scattering clumps of grass in its wake.

I looked at Shadamar and wondered why I thought I could defeat him.

You are stubborn, Sion said. *And you don't listen to me.*

Sometimes I do.

Not when it matters. Run. Please.

I looked Sion in the eyes and slowly shook my head. "I'm tired of running." Turning back to face Shadamar, I tightened my grip on the hilt of my blade. Every second I kept his attention was another opportunity for Maren and the other sorcerers to get the barrier back up.

"Let's finish this," I spat, lunging forward. We clashed in a flurry of blows, but Shadamar was as agile as a feline, dodging every one of my strikes with ease. It was as though he could guess what I was going to do before I did it.

He's reading your body language, Sion said. *Don't be so obvious about what you're going to do.*

I considered her words. He had more battle experience and was using his magic to augment himself, but that didn't mean he couldn't be defeated. Something Katori once said to me suddenly echoed in my mind: *Amidst chaos, there is always a chance for success.*

Shadamar was reading my movements, but what if I could trick him? I feigned left and went right, dodging his sword and thrusting my blade at his leg. The tip of my sword struck him and cut a gash in his thigh, surprising both of us.

In the blink of an eye, his hold on Sion slipped and she scrambled up, swiping at him with her claws. He backpedaled, cursing as blood soaked his pant leg. I pressed my advantage, hacking and slashing wildly. With every step he took, blood spurted from his wound. He roared in pain as he parried my strikes, but before I could land another hit, he unleashed a torrent of dark energy, engulfing me in shadows.

My vision blurred, and I stumbled backward, swinging my blade to ward off an attack. None came. When the darkness cleared, Shadamar was gone.

17

Where did he go?

Sion's tail flicked behind her as she gazed around the battlefield. *There.* She bounded away, leaving battered soldiers in her wake. I sprinted after her, the ground trembling beneath my feet as she ran.

We need to catch him before he escapes, she said. *The barrier is forming.*

I glanced back and saw the air rippling with magic. I pushed my legs harder, holding my sword behind me. Sion leaped into the air, gliding over the wreckage of a toppled war machine. I went around it, dodging enemies to keep up with Sion.

She spun about, crashing her tail into a swarm of soldiers. They went flying in every direction, and she pounced on Shadamar, pinning him to the ground with her claws. Magic flared from him, and Sion screeched in pain, but she didn't release him. I slowed to a jog as I got closer and jabbed the tip of my sword against Shadamar's throat.

"You've lost," I huffed, out of breath. "Surrender."

"You think that if you kill me you win?" He laughed, madness in his eyes. "I am nothing compared to what's coming."

I stared at him, unsure what he meant.

"Do it," he snarled. "Kill me. Kill me like you killed my brother!"

My nerve faltered, and I looked at Sion. She kept her focus on Shadamar.

Let's go, I told her. *The barrier will take care of him.*

He deserves to die.

And he will. He has caused suffering using his magic, and now magic will end his life.

I removed my sword from his neck. Sion didn't move. I could feel her hatred burning through the bond.

You said yourself we need to hurry. The barrier is expanding.

The air hummed as magic flowed into the barrier. The battle raged on, and no one paid any heed to the impending doom.

As soon as I let go, he will use his dark magic against us.

I had the same thought, but maybe we can take flight before he gets a spell off.

Remove his tongue, Sion said.

He can still cast spells with hand gestures. I've seen him do it.

Then cut off his hands, too.

I hesitated, knowing it was a ruthless tactic, but the urgency of the situation made me consider it. We had to survive, and I knew Shadamar would stop at nothing to kill us. I knelt and grabbed Shadamar's right arm, pulling it free from under Sion's claw.

"You're just a pawn in someone else's game," he hissed.

"Maybe, but pawns can still win." I brought my sword down as hard as I could, severing his hand from his arm.

Surprisingly, Shadamar didn't cry out. He forced his eyes shut and his body tremored, but no sound escaped his lips. It was a gruesome act, and I despised doing it, but it had to be done. Moving to the other side, I cut his other hand off. Blood gushed from his wounds unabated, drenching the ground around him.

Now his tongue, Sion demanded.

The thought of doing that made me queasy. *I can't. This is enough. Come on, let's get out of here.*

Shadamar's body went limp, and his head lolled to the side.

He's no threat to anyone unconscious, I said.

Satisfied, Sion lifted her claw. Shadamar remained where he was, lifeless except for his erratic breathing and the rise and fall of his chest. I wiped my sword off and sheathed it, then climbed up Sion's shoulder and into the saddle. She took to the air.

"To the Citadel!" I shouted as we flew over the battlefield. "Riders, return to the Citadel!"

Whether they ignored me or just couldn't hear over the din of battle, nobody retreated. The Valgaardians had routed the royal riders, and the army below was in disarray. I felt lightheaded as magic teased my mind, and Anesko's voice echoed in my thoughts.

Flee the battlefield while you can. The barrier will seal anything in its path. Stay at your own peril!

The vertigo faded, and I held on to the saddle as Sion swooped around and sped across the sky to get beyond the barrier's reach. Once we were out of harm's way, she slowed her pace and we watched as the barrier closed over the battlefield, enveloping most of the enemy's forces.

The barrier was a sight to behold—a shimmering wall of energy that was as tall as it was wide. I couldn't fathom the amount of magic that powered the spell. It remained in place for a moment before slowly shrinking. It consumed everything it touched, leaving the ground scorched and ruined.

Screams erupted as the barrier burned people alive, turning them to ash. Sion and I watched grimly as the magic ravaged the battlefield, silencing the cries for help and leaving nothing but glowing embers and dust behind. Even the trebuchets and ballista were scorched from existence.

The aftermath of the barrier's destruction was horrifying. Sion and I hovered over the swath of destruction, unable to turn away from the scene. As we flew over the now desolate battlefield, I vainly searched for Shadamar's remains, but there was nothing left. An entire army had been erased in mere moments. Sion offered comfort through the bond as emotions overwhelmed me.

What have we done?

We did what was necessary.

We had no choice. That's what I told myself, over and over. The cost was high, but the loss of life was necessary.

I hope this never happens again, I said.

No one knows what the future holds, but I do not foresee things going this way a second time. This will serve as a warning to our enemies. The arena of war is a playground for sorcerers.

As we flew back to the Citadel, I couldn't help but wonder how many innocent people had been caught in the crossfire. Despite everything Shadamar had done, I couldn't shake the feeling that we were no better than the monsters we fought against. We had survived, and the balance of power had shifted in our favor. What we did with that power would reveal if we truly were monsters.

I prayed we weren't.

18

As the days turned to weeks, the battle felt more like a dream than a reality, but the charred field in front of the Citadel was a constant reminder that it had truly happened. The mercenaries that Altin had sent arrived after the battle was over. It turned out their leader was Seren Gray, the mercenary I'd met back in Tiradale. She had been Geoff's employer, the man I'd worked for when I first found Sion.

Just as Altin had assumed, she was eager to help. Her former days as a rider may have been long gone, but her sense of loyalty remained. She and her band set out to track down the soldiers who'd escaped the battle. Their fate was in her hands now, and I suspected she would not be very forgiving.

I sighed and closed the book I was reading, setting it on top of the growing pile to my right. Now that one problem had been solved, it was time to deal with the next one. Bryngar had said that the dragon slayers were from a land beyond the sea. So far, I had yet to find anything useful about where it might be located. I stood and stretched, rubbing my lower back where an ache throbbed from sitting too long.

"Bryngar said he sent a message to them, yet he doesn't know where they are," I said, looking at Maren. She was sitting at the desk across from mine, also flipping through books for clues.

"Yes. I asked him about that. He said he used some sort of spherical item to send the message. I'm certain it's magical in nature, but that doesn't help us. You don't need to know where someone is physically to communicate with them, but it is limited by distance. Somehow, this item isn't affected by that. It takes extreme focus and a lot of energy to send a message from here to Valgaard. I can't imagine the amount of magic it would take to send something across the sea."

"I haven't found anything that indicates there are lands anywhere beyond the sea, but that doesn't mean anything. I mean, we found that old royal outpost when we sailed to find the wild dragons, so I'm sure there are other lands out there."

"We already know there are," Maren said. "Remember when we saw the elven and dwarven souls on the ferry?"

My eyes widened. "I forgot all about that! You're right. Now that I think about it, there was an elf who said dragons were servants in his land. Do you remember that?"

"I do. We aren't trying to find elves or dwarves, though. The dragon slayers were humans."

"True."

I walked to one of the tall windows and stared out at the courtyard below. The sun was setting, bathing the sky in hues of orange and scarlet. The western side of the school had suffered significant damage during the battle, and rubble still littered the area around it. Anesko said the repairs were going to take a few months. His injuries healed well, and he was back to normal.

"If the dragon slayers bring an army with them, we'll have to leave the Citadel behind," I said. "We don't have the strength or the numbers to fight another war."

"The Order can be rebuilt," Maren replied. "And Bryngar said he will do whatever he can to stop them from coming here. We have to trust things will work out."

"Yes, but we should plan for what happens if they do not."

Silence fell between us, and I turned to face her.

"When does this end? When do we get to make a life for ourselves instead of worrying about everyone else?"

"What are you talking about, Eldwin? This *is* our life. We're riders. It is our duty to live selflessly."

I rubbed my face. She was right. It was my exhaustion speaking. "Sorry," I muttered. "I should probably get some rest."

"I'll come with you," Maren replied, closing her book and standing.

She grabbed my hand, and we walked the empty halls together back to our room. My life had gone down a very different path than I ever expected, but I couldn't complain. I had found Sion on this path—and Maren—and I knew deep down that we had to continue on this journey. There was no room for selfish desires.

Despite the constant dangers and challenges we faced, we had done it together. We had saved countless lives, and there was no doubt our sacrifices had made a difference. Whatever tomorrow brought, we would face it together, side by side, as riders.

As family.

THE END OF BOOK 15

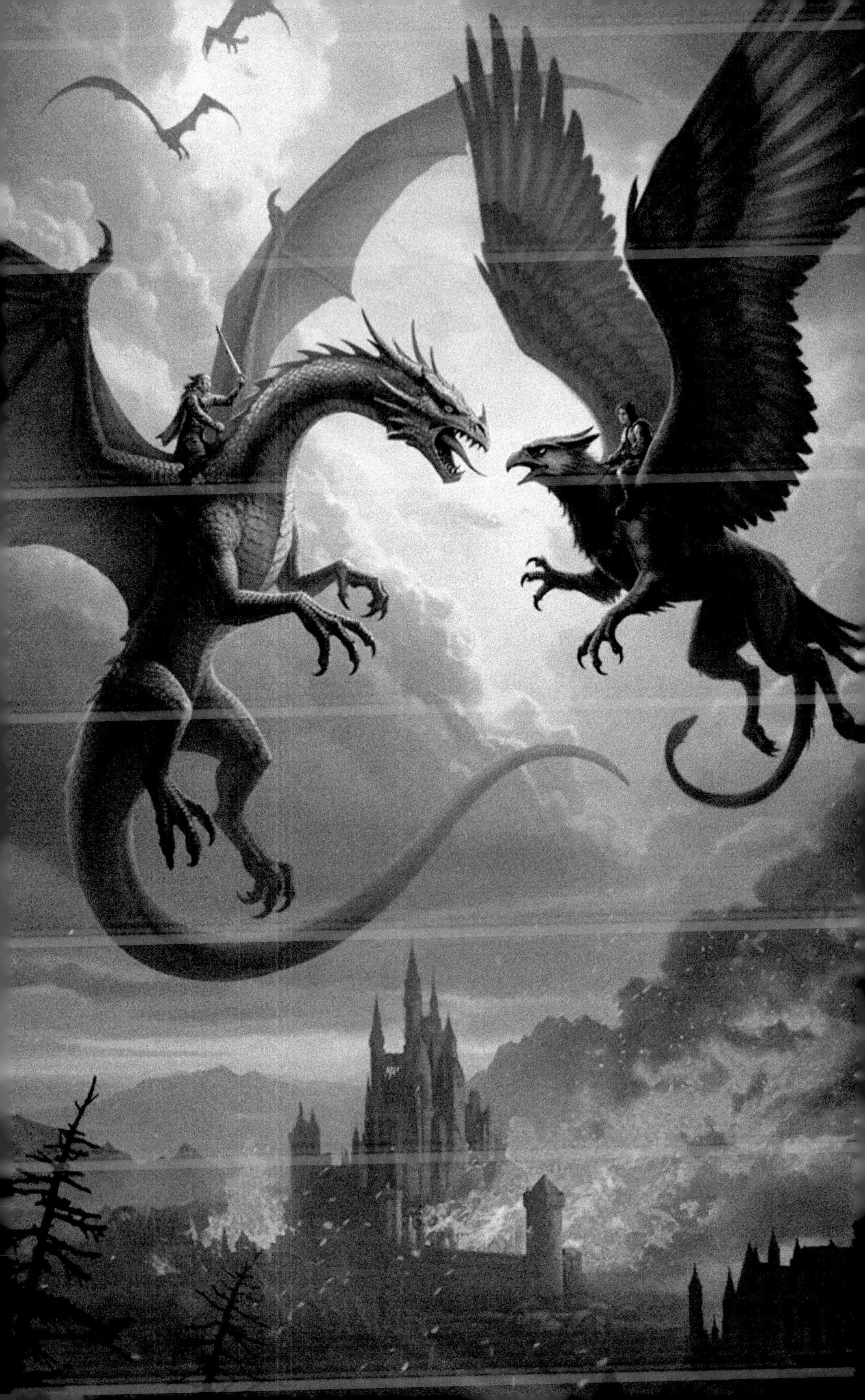

Wings
of the
Fallen

1

THE CLANG OF STEEL RANG out as Matthias Baines parried a mock blow. The training grounds of the Citadel were alive with the din of combat, each member honing their skills against constructed foes made of straw and wood. Matthias ducked and weaved between his adversaries, his sword a blur of motion. Sweat glistened on his brow, and the early morning sun cast slanted shadows across the courtyard where the riders trained.

"Keep your guard up, Alton!" Matthias called out.

He pivoted on his heel, dispatching another imaginary enemy with a decisive thrust. His fellow guards rallied to the call, their formation tight as they pushed forward, advancing against an unseen force.

"Form up," he commanded sharply.

Together, they moved as one entity, their shields interlocking with one another. Matthias's ice blue eyes scanned the field. A wooden adversary charged, its mechanism whirring. With a shout, he broke rank, engaging the construct with a series of swift strikes that left it dismantled on the ground.

"Enough!"

The booming voice cut through the fray, halting the clatter of weapons and the shouts of exertion. Curate Aric, a towering figure clad in burnished armor, strode onto the field. His gaze swept over the riders, all of them panting and looking at him expectantly.

"Matthias," Aric said, his eyes locking onto the man. Matthias straightened, his chest heaving as he awaited the curate's judgment. "Your performance today was exceptional. You've shown not just skill but the heart of a true dragon rider. Bravery and loyalty are the pillars upon which our brotherhood stands, and you, lad, have them in spades."

Pride swelled within Matthias's chest, and a warmth that combated the chill of the morning air swept over him. Curate Aric's praise was not given lightly, and to receive such commendation from a man he admired stirred something within him he hadn't felt since the birth of his son.

"Thank you, sir," Matthias replied breathlessly, adrenaline still coursing through his veins. "I serve at the pleasure of the Order and the Citadel."

"Indeed, you do." Aric's stern expression softened into a rare smile as he placed a heavy hand on Matthias's shoulder. "Keep this up, and I foresee a bright future for you within our ranks."

Around them, the other guards nodded in agreement, their faces etched with respect and a hint of envy. Matthias felt the weight of their expectations, but it was a burden he was ready to bear. He had vowed to protect the kingdom and his fellow riders, and it was not an oath he took lightly. But more than that, he wanted his wife and son to be proud of him and his accomplishments.

"Back to it, then," Curate Aric commanded, releasing Matthias.

With a final nod, Matthias rejoined his companions. He resumed his exercise, his movements full of renewed vigor.

—

Matthias's muscles ached with a satisfying burn as he strode toward the stable. He nodded to the men on watch at the entrance of the underground cave and continued inside, the stone beneath his boots rough and uneven. The clash of swords and the shouts of training exercises faded behind him, replaced by the calmer sounds of dragons stirring within their caves.

Hello Valkyra, Matthias greeted as he approached his dragon's alcove. Her blue scales glittered under the torchlight, making it appear as though she were glowing. At the sound of his voice, the dragon lifted her head, her piercing eyes focusing on him.

Matthias extended a hand to gently stroke the smooth ridge of her snout. Valkyra responded with a low rumble that resonated through the air, vibrating against Matthias's palm. They shared a moment of quiet understanding, a silent conversation between rider and dragon, each basking in the other's presence.

Valkyra nuzzled his hand, her breath warm. She had been more than just a mount to Matthias; she was his companion, his confidant, the wings upon which his courage soared. Together they had forged an unbreakable bond through trials and triumphs alike. He loved Valkyra, dearly so. He loved his family, too, but the love he had for Valkyra was something else entirely.

Their tranquil moment was shattered by the urgent tolling of the Citadel's belltower. A deep, sonorous sound that signaled imminent danger. Matthias stiffened, his heart racing as he recognized the call to arms—an alarm not heard in years.

One of the guards from outside rushed into view. "The border villages are under siege!"

"By who?" Matthias asked.

"Midia!"

Curate Aric entered the stable, his stern expression silently reprimanding the guard's panicked news.

"Saddle up," Aric ordered. "We leave immediately."

The stable erupted into chaos. Matthias grabbed Valkyra's harness from the hook on the wall and began strapping it onto her.

Are you ready? he asked.

I am always ready.

Valkyra spread her wings wide, knocking over a stack of hay. She reared up slightly, her body tensing like a coiled spring.

Matthias secured the last buckle and hoisted himself onto her back. His gaze swept over the flurry of activity around them. The riders were mobilizing with impressive speed, each of them driven by the same sense of duty that coursed within him.

Valkyra stomped out of the stable and into the courtyard, issuing a thunderous roar. The clarion call was answered by several other dragons, and Matthias's heart thundered in his chest, mirroring the heavy footsteps of dragons that soon filled the air. His fellow riders were a whirlwind of motion around him, each one armed with a lance or a sword. Matthias's own blade was sheathed at his waist, the weight of it providing a small measure of comfort.

Valkyra snorted, a plume of smoke rising from her nostrils. Her scales gleamed like polished sapphires under the sunlight, and Matthias couldn't help but admire his dragon's beauty.

"Move out!" Aric shouted, redirecting his focus.

With a powerful leap, Valkyra surged into the sky, which became a maelstrom of color and sound as the other riders took flight. They realigned mid-air, getting into formation. Matthias gripped the saddle horn tightly and turned his gaze toward the border.

While he was glad for the excitement, he prayed they weren't going to war.

THE SKY WAS A CACOPHONY of flapping wings and roars. Smoke billowed up from the ground, the land scorched by dragon flame. The Midians had soldiers on the ground and in the air, and their griffons shrieked loudly as they battled with the Osnen riders.

Valkyra banked sharply to the left, passing near a group of griffons. Matthias's sword sliced through the air, finding its mark in the gaps of an enemy's armor. The soldier's eyes widened in surprise before he slipped free of the saddle and fell to his death. Matthias's short brown hair was matted with sweat and grime, sticking to his forehead beneath his helmet. He deftly parried a lance aimed for his chest, countering with a thrust that sent the man backward, crashing hard against the back of his griffon.

Around him, the battle raged on, the riders outnumbered but holding their own. With every beat of her powerful wings, Valkyra weaved through the aerial melee, her fiery breath carving paths of destruction through the enemy's forces. The smell of burnt flesh stung Matthias's nostrils, but he ignored the stench and continued striking at any enemy who came within range.

"Hold the line!" Curate Aric shouted, his voice cutting through the din.

Matthias was glad to be fighting by the man's side. Even as the odds stacked ever higher against them, Aric's resolve did not waver. His dragon moved with a grace that belied his bulk, each slash of his claws measured and precise, conserving energy for the long fight ahead. Aric's movements were equally deadly, honed through years of rigorous training, now on full display as he defended not just his own life but the lives of his brothers-in-arms.

They need help, Valkyra said.

Matthias scanned the ground and spotted a few people fleeing, a contingent of Midian soldiers chasing after them. He eyed the formation of the riders and was confident they wouldn't be overtaken if he broke away.

Take us down, he told Valkyra.

She tucked her wings in and sped toward the ground, pulling up at the last moment. Matthias leaped from the saddle and hit the ground running, intercepting the soldiers. He dodged a spray of earth as Valkyra landed heavily nearby, her claws gouging deep furrows in the soil. Matthias drove back an opponent who had sought to exploit the momentary distraction.

His bravery was not just for show, nor was it reckless. He sought to protect the innocent, and he feared if the Midians won here, they would rampage across Osnen unchecked before the Citadel rallied the rest of the riders. That thought drove him onward, and he dispatched three men before Valkyra flamed the rest.

The people who fled were safely away, and he climbed back into the saddle just as a cry sliced through the cacophony of battle. Matthias turned sharply, his gaze locking onto the source. Curate Aric and his dragon had landed on the ground and a group of Midian soldiers were converging on them. The seasoned rider fought valiantly, but the press of bodies threatened to overwhelm him, and his dragon was beset on all sides.

Without hesitation, Matthias mentally shouted to Valkyra, *To Aric, now!*

The dragon responded instantly, her powerful muscles propelling them forward with breathtaking speed. She bounded ahead, talons outstretched, and snatched a foe about to strike Aric. With a twist of her mighty neck, the threat was neutralized, the soldier tossed aside like a rag doll.

"Riders, to me!" Matthias bellowed, rallying the others even as he fought. They responded to the call, their dragons descending in a protective formation around the Curate.

"Good work," Aric grunted, acknowledging the save with a terse nod before turning to engage an attacker.

"We're not done yet," Matthias called back. They worked together, a storm of wings and valor, a tempest that would not be easily quelled.

A collective roar thundered from the throats of both rider and dragon alike, a sound that melded with the clashing swords and the whooshing of great leathery wings. For a fleeting moment, the tide of battle seemed to turn in their favor as the enemy's advance faltered.

"Push them back!" Aric cried, his voice rising above the clash of arms. His call was met with a surge of concerted effort, riders ushering their dragons into the heart of the fray, flames and steel rending the air. Valkyra's fiery breath cleared a path through the encroaching forces, allowing Aric to rally and orchestrate a counter-offensive.

Matthias could feel hope burgeoning within, a sensation that lifted his spirits even as sweat and grime streaked his face. Valkyra shared in the sentiment, her emotions flooding their bond.

But the reprieve was short-lived.

The enemy, cunning and relentless, had not been idle. As the smoke from Valkyra's breath dissipated, it revealed the Midian forces regrouping with unnerving discipline, their numbers seemingly undiminished. They charged once more, a wave that sought to overwhelm the riders with sheer brute force.

This time, the clash was catastrophic. The ground trembled beneath the onslaught, and the sky darkened with the shadow of the Midian's griffon reinforcements. Matthias fought with a fervor born of desperation, his sword a blur of motion as he parried and struck with lethal precision. Yet for every enemy that fell, two took their place.

He witnessed a fellow rider pulled from the saddle, a cry of anguish lost amidst the chaos. Anger burned within Matthias, fueling his resolve. He wanted to avenge those who had fallen, but this was no mere battle—it was a fight for their very lives.

"For every life they take, we shall repay tenfold!" Matthias yelled.

Valkyra echoed his defiance with a resounding roar, her flames lashing out with renewed ferocity. But even as they fought, the realization that they were being pushed back, inch by harrowing inch, settled heavily upon Matthias's shoulders. He refused to let it break his spirit.

"Fall back!" Aric bellowed. "Riders, fall back!"

Matthias dispatched another enemy and Valkyra flapped her powerful wings as she leaped into the air, quickly ascending above the battlefield. Below, the village now bore the scars of war, its fate hanging in the balance. He knew they could not relent, not while a single breath remained in them to fight.

Smoke unfurled like ghastly ribbons, and Valkyra's wings cut through the acrid air, each beat a somber drumroll to the village's dirge. Matthias's hands tightened on the reins, his knuckles white as bone against the black leather. Below them, a marketplace had become a roaring inferno, wood and thatch crackling fiercely as the flames consumed them.

"By the gods..." Matthias muttered, his voice barely a whisper.

He could see the silhouettes of dragons against the blaze, desperately trying to stem the tide of Midia's relentless troops. They were like an unending sea of darkness.

"Matthias!" The call came from Larke, a fellow rider whose face was smeared with soot and blood, her expression a grim mask that mirrored his own. "The eastern barricade won't hold!"

His gaze followed her outstretched arm, witnessing the collapse of a defensive wall as Midia's forces poured through the breach like floodwaters through a shattered dam. A cottage crumbled beneath the onslaught, its timbers groaning in protest before succumbing to the violent assault, sending up a plume of ash and embers.

"Retreat!" Aric roared, his command cutting through the turmoil.

A guttural cry rent the air, and Matthias's blood ran cold. He watched helplessly as a dragon and its rider spiraled downwards, their bond severed by a well-aimed spear. The ground rushed up to meet them in a sickening embrace, and Matthias felt something within him shatter.

"Thane," he whispered, the name of his fallen comrade a bitter taste on his lips.

Grief clawed at his chest, a searing pain that rivaled the heat of the very fires that raged below. Thane, who had laughed beside him during their training, who had sworn the same oaths of protection and service to their people, now lay broken amidst the ruins.

"Matthias!" It was Aric's commanding voice that pierced his sorrow, a beacon calling him back to the present. "We must retreat to the Citadel!"

"Retreat?" Matthias echoed, the word foreign, anathema to all he believed in. Yet even as he rebelled against it, he saw the truth etched in the smoke-filled skies: the village was lost.

"We will avenge you," Matthias vowed silently, the vow a promise to those who would no longer rise into the sky. "All of you."

With a heavy heart, he urged Valkyra to follow Curate Aric's orders, their path now one of survival. As they withdrew, the cries of the dying mingled with the roar of dragons, a chorus of agony and defiance that would haunt Matthias long after the battle's end.

"Look out!" Larke's warning cry came just in time. Valkyra veered sharply as a barrage of arrows came towards them, missing her wings by mere inches. Larke's dragon, Icaron, swooped down, incinerating the archers with a blast of flames.

"Close one," Matthias said, offering a quick nod of thanks to her.

"Too close," Larke replied, her eyes scanning the ground for more threats.

Their retreat took them to the safety of the Citadel's high walls, where the remaining dragons landed in the courtyard. The mighty group was now but a shadow of its former self, their numbers half of what they were, faces etched with fatigue and loss.

"Circle up!" Curate Aric's voice boomed across the yard, bringing the scattered riders together. His gaze swept over them, taking in every bruise, every dent in their armor. "We've been dealt a grave blow this day, but there will be time to mourn later."

"We cannot let Midia claim any more ground," Matthias said. Valkyra growled in agreement. "We have to strike back—"

"Strategically," Aric finished for him, the words a reprimand. "Yes, we will retaliate. But first, we need a strategy, one that turns the tide in our favor. I will speak with Master Pevus and the other Curates. For now, everyone should get some rest. I have no doubt we'll need it."

Murmurs of assent rippled through the group, yet doubt lingered in the air like the smoke that had chased them from the battlefield. The riders dispersed, some to tend to their dragons, others to seek the solace of rest. Matthias dismounted and turned his gaze to the horizon where the last light of day bled into darkness.

Midia has not seen the last of us, Matthias told Valkyra.

3

THE NEXT MORNING, MATTHIAS AWOKE early. He went to the training ground and practiced alone. His sleep had been restless, and now he took his frustrations out on the straw dummies. He should have done more, fought harder. The image of Thane falling played continuously in his mind, adding force to his strikes. When he grew tired, he threw his sword down and used the back of his hand to wipe the sweat from his brow.

"Matthias!" a voice called out, echoing throughout the empty courtyard. Matthias turned to see a small group approaching. The one who'd called his name, Curate Henrik, smiled broadly at him. He clasped Matthias on the shoulder in a grip that was both congratulatory and bone-crushing.

"Your valor in battle is becoming the stuff of songs!"

"Only doing my duty, Curate," Matthias replied, the corners of his mouth lifting into a modest smile, even as his chest was heavy with loss. He could feel the weight of eyes upon him, each gaze carrying its own measure of respect.

"Modest as always," Curate Serah chuckled, her dark eyes twinkling with mirth. She stepped forward, offering a respectful nod.

"We heard the stories of your feats yesterday—like a tempest unleashed. You helped save many people. You've earned every bit of praise."

"Thank you, Curate," Matthias said, his spirits lifting. Perhaps he was being too hard on himself.

Curate Aric severed the throng of riders with decisive strides. Matthias's spine stiffened at the sight of him.

"Matthias Baines," Aric's voice resonated with the authority that had weathered countless battles. "Your valor yesterday has not gone unnoticed."

Matthias snapped to attention, his heart hammering in his chest against his ribs. The respect he held for Aric was etched into his very posture, every fiber of his being radiating attentiveness. Aric's gaze swept over him, as if assessing the mettle that had brought Matthias from lowly birth to the vaulted ranks of the Dragon Guard.

"Walk with me," he said, a subtle tilt of his head indicating a more private corner of the courtyard away from prying ears.

They moved in tandem, their boots echoing against stone, until they were shrouded by the shadow of a looming spire. Here, Aric's demeanor shifted, the mask of command giving way to earnest gravity. He leaned closer, and Matthias could smell the leather and steel that clung to the Curate like a second skin.

"Your courage is without question," Aric began in a lowered voice, his eyes searching Matthias's. "But it is your loyalty that I must now call upon. The attack yesterday was orchestrated by Valerius Draven. He proclaims himself king, but he's nothing more than fake royalty. He's taken over Midia, and he poses a great threat to our realm."

Matthias nodded, his jaw set. Now he had a name to direct his anger towards. His hand involuntarily clenched.

"I hope you'll understand the gravity of what I am about to ask. We need intelligence—eyes within enemy lines. Someone to gather information on Valerious's next move."

A flicker of surprise darted across Matthias's face. "You wish... for *me* to undertake this mission?"

"Indeed." Aric gave a slight nod. "It will be perilous. Subterfuge and stealth must be your allies. What you learn could turn the tide of this impending war."

The sun broke over the wall, dissolving the cool embrace of the shadows. Matthias felt the enormity of the task settle upon his shoulders, yet there was no hesitation in his voice when he responded. "I will not fail you, nor the Order."

"Very good," Aric said, a flicker of pride crossing his face. From within his cloak, he produced a sealed scroll. "This contains all you need to know. Depart tonight under the cover of darkness, and may the wind guide you."

Matthias took the scroll, the parchment rough against his fingers. The journey ahead would be a path fraught with danger, but he would tread unflinchingly for the sake of duty.

"You aim to dance with the shadows," a female voice said. Matthias saw Evelyn approaching, one of their physicians. She joined them and smiled. "Even the most adept dancer needs a partner. Curate," she greeted Aric with a nod.

She had been a close friend to Matthias, even before coming to the Citadel. In another life, she may have even been more than that. Her hair was blonde and straight, though it was currently tied back in a ribbon, and her eyes were a striking blue.

"Your healing skills are unmatched," Aric said. "But this task will be perilous. It requires a warrior."

"Which is why you need me to go with him," Evelyn persisted. "Who better to tend wounds in the field than a healer? Besides," she added, her lips curling into a grin as she looked at Matthias. "You need someone to watch your back."

Matthias hesitated, torn between the instinct to protect her and the knowledge that her abilities could mean the difference between life and death. He studied her defiant posture and the look in her eyes and saw more than just a healer; he saw a warrior not unlike himself.

"Your aid would be invaluable," he admitted, glancing at Aric. "But if harm befell her—"

"Then my blood is not on your hands," Evelyn interjected firmly. "I know the risks."

The conviction of her tone brooked no argument, and something in Matthias's heart yielded. He knew he would be stronger with her at his side.

"A companion would be nice," he conceded. "So long as Curate Aric approves?"

They both turned their eyes to him. "It is safer to travel in pairs, and it may help you to keep unwanted attention by appearing as a couple… so long as you don't have any duties pending, I'll speak with Master Pevus and let him know I approved it."

"All of my usual tasks are complete," Evelyn confirmed.

"Very well. Remember, you are to gather information and report back. Don't try to battle the whole of Midia on your own."

Matthias nodded. "Understood."

4

ONCE NIGHT HAD FALLEN AND stars pierced the night sky, Matthias met Evelyn in the stable. The scent of hay and dragon musk greeted him, and Valkyra touched his mind as he neared her cave.

Did you get plenty to eat? It might be a while before you have a decent meal.

Valkyra rumbled softly, the sound reverberating off the walls. *I have known hunger before. Do not worry about me.*

Matthias ran a hand along Valkyra's snout. She snorted affectionately, steam rising from her nostrils into the cool air. He checked the saddle straps for any signs of strain while Evelyn packed salves and bandages into the saddlebags. She glanced at him, her blue eyes reflecting the torchlight.

He felt her eyes but ignored her, focusing his attention on running a steel file along one of Valkyra's talons to remove a spur.

I tried chewing that off but it was too small, she said.

Finished with the talon, Matthias hoisted himself onto Valkyra's broad back, careful to distribute his weight evenly. He took a moment to settle in place, adjusting the straps of his saddle. The dragon let out a contented rumble, her enormous wings shifting slightly against her sides. Evelyn followed suit, situating herself behind Matthias.

"You ready?" he asked.

"As ready as I'll ever be," Evelyn replied.

Valkyra exited the cave and headed up the slope that took them into the courtyard. The crisp night air sent a shiver down Matthias's back, and Evelyn stifled her giggle. As the dragon walked, the clinking of Matthia's armor punctuated the stillness of the night. The dragon reached the center of the courtyard and tensed her legs, then pushed off, launching them skyward with a gust of wind that sent loose pebbles skittering across the cobblestones.

The Citadel fell away below as they ascended, its stone walls shrinking until there was nothing visible amidst the shadows. They were in the open expanse of the night sky, and Matthias lost himself in the cadence of the rhythmic beat of Valkyra's wings.

Evelyn's arms tightened around his waist. "Do you see anything below?" she asked, her voice barely audible over the wind.

Matthias scanned the dark landscape beneath them, searching for any signs of movement or light that might indicate enemy activity. The fields stretched out like a black ocean, broken only by the occasional cluster of trees or distant homestead.

Your eyes are sharper than mine, he said to Valkyra. *Do you see anything to be concerned about?*

The ground is clear.

"Nothing," Matthias called out over his shoulder.

They flew for several hours, passing over the ruins of the town they'd tried to save and across the border into Midia. The canopy of stars stretched endlessly above them, while the shapes of the world below melded into shades of darkness and light. Matthias's gaze remained fixed ahead, his eyelids growing heavy.

As the light of dawn tinged the horizon with color, Evelyn finally broke the silence. "We need to land away from prying eyes, somewhere no one will see your dragon."

Matthias shook off his sleepiness and nodded. A cluster of lights appeared below; a village slowly waking to life. Matthias gestured toward it, and Evelyn followed his line of sight.

"It's as good a place as any to gather information."

Take us down but stay out of range of the town. Evelyn and I will continue ahead on foot.

Valkyra touched down on the outskirts in a heavily wooded area. Matthias dismounted, his boots sinking softly into the dew-covered grass. He offered his hand to Evelyn and helped her down.

Matthias placed a hand on Valkyra's snout. *Stay hidden. If anything happens, fly back to Osnen.*

Valkyra's eyes narrowed, and a puff of warm air escaped her nostrils. *I will not leave you behind,* the dragon replied.

I know you won't, but I'm still going to tell you to anyway. We'll be back as soon as possible.

He patted her scales and turned to Evelyn. "Let's find an inn. We'll get something to eat and keep our ears up."

Together, they walked through the woods toward the town. The sun crested over the hills, casting its warm glow upon them and driving away the chill in Matthias's bones.

The town was a sorry sight. Low, weathered buildings leaned against one another like weary travelers, and the streets were little more than packed dirt, muddied from a recent rain. Smoke rose from a number of the dwellings, and the few people they passed barely acknowledged them.

The inn was located in the center of the town. Its shutters hung crookedly, and a worn sign in front depicted a caravan winding through the mountains. The faded words "The Caravan's Rest" were barely legible.

Matthias pushed open the door, holding it for Evelyn. Inside, the common room was dimly lit by a handful of lanterns and the flickering glow of a hearth. Patrons hunched over their food, their voices low and wary, and the air was thick with the scent of wood smoke and roasted meat.

They found a table by the fire and waited for the innkeeper. A burly man with a salt-and-pepper beard approached, smiling broadly.

"Welcome to my humble establishment," he greeted. "What can I get for you fine travelers?"

"Do you have any rooms available?" Matthias asked.

"Aye, but just one."

Matthias glanced at Evelyn, who nodded her approval.

"We'll take it. And two of your best meals, whatever that might be."

The innkeeper nodded and left, returning shortly with two steaming plates of food. Matthias's mouth watered at the sight of fluffy biscuits smothered in gravy, sausages as long as his fingers, and a heaping pile of scrambled eggs. He took a bite of the biscuit, and the savory, meaty flavor of the gravy danced on his tongue. Matthias savored each bite while listening in to the conversations of the other patrons.

One in particular caught his attention, though it was less a conversation and more an old man raving to himself.

"…dark magic. He's using dark magic to control them, I tell you. They aren't meant to be bent to no man's will." His raspy voice carried the weight of someone who'd seen too much. "The False King," he continued, his hands trembling as he clutched his mug. "His army is going to destroy everything. He'll enslave the great beasts for his evil purposes. It isn't natural."

"I've told you before to stop rambling nonsense in here," the innkeeper said as he walked over to the table the old man was sitting at. "You're scaring my customers."

The man seemed to suddenly realize where he was and mumbled something, casting his gaze around the room.

Evelyn leaned closer to Matthias. "What do you think he's talking about?"

Matthias didn't answer immediately, his brow furrowed in thought as he ate the last of his food. He slid the plate aside and wiped his mouth with his hand.

"There's only one way to find out."

5

AFTER THE INNKEEPER HANDED OVER the key to their room, Matthias watched the old man carefully, waiting for him to leave. When he finally staggered out of the inn, Matthias and Evelyn followed, keeping their distance. The old man shuffled down the muddy street, muttering under his breath.

When they were far enough from prying eyes, Matthias quickened his pace and called out, "Excuse me, sir. Can we speak with you?"

The old man whirled around, his eyes wild with fear. "Stay back! I know what you are—agents of the False King, sent to silence me!"

Matthias held up his hands in a gesture of peace. "We're not here to harm you. We just want to know more about what you were saying in the inn."

The man's gaze darted between Matthias and Evelyn. "How do I know I can trust you?"

"Because if we were with the False King, you'd already be dead," Matthias said.

The old man hesitated, then nodded slowly. "Fair enough. Not here." He glanced around uneasily. "Too many ears." He led them to a secluded alley, glancing over his shoulder to make sure they weren't followed.

"Tell us everything," Matthias said.

The old man took a deep breath, his eyes shifting nervously. "I escaped from Araphel. I've been a servant there most of my life. The False King... he's using dark magic, experimenting with things no one should ever mess with. He's trying to craft a spell that will bend dragons to his will. It's unnatural, I tell you. He plans to invade Osnen by turning the dragons against their riders."

Matthias and Evelyn exchanged a grim look.

"Do you know when he plans to invade Osnen?"

"As soon as he figures out the spell. Between himself and his sorcerer, it can't be long now."

"How difficult would it be to catch him alone?" Matthias asked.

"The False King? Impossible, I tell you. An army resides at Araphel, and his sorcerer has eyes everywhere." The old man shuddered. "If you had an army of your own, you might have a chance, but even still, you'll need a weapon he can't defend against."

Matthias's mind raced as he absorbed the man's words. The gravity of the situation weighed heavily upon him, knowing that the False King's intentions could bring ruin to Osnen and its people.

"We need to find a way to stop him," Evelyn said.

"There might just be a way, if you're brave enough." The old man lowered his voice and motioned them closer. Matthias scrunched his nose as the stench of sour ale assaulted him.

"There is a place hidden in the mountains beyond Araphel. It's said to hold a weapon of immense power, one that could even defeat the False King's magic."

"What kind of weapon?" Matthias asked, his curiosity piqued.

"A sword forged for the first king of Midia," the old man whispered. "They say it can cleave through enchantments and strike down the mightiest of foes."

"Where can we find this sword?"

"In the ruins of Valen," the old man answered. "But beware, for many have entered seeking its power and never returned."

Matthias thanked him for the information and slipped him a few coins.

"Good luck, rider of Osnen. You'll need it."

"Who said I was a dragon rider?"

"When you've lived as long as I have, there isn't much that escapes your notice."

The man shuffled away, leaving them in the alley.

"We need to warn the Order," Evelyn said. "If the False King manages to control our dragons, the entire kingdom will be in peril."

"We need to find this sword, *then* we can return to inform the Order."

"The False King could launch his attack before we find it. With no warning… it would be a slaughter."

"What good is a warning if we don't have a way to fight back? We need the sword."

"He could have made up the tale of that sword," Evelyn said. "We don't know anything about him."

Matthias clenched his jaw. He was reminded of why nothing had ever happened between them. She constantly challenged him.

"If you want to go back, I'll have Valkyra take you. But I'm staying."

"I'm not leaving you here by yourself, Matthias."

"Then I guess you're coming with me."

They engaged in a staring contest until Evelyn relented. "Fine. We'll do this your way. If the sword doesn't exist, you've wasted our time. And if Osnen is invaded while we're digging around in some blasted ruins, the blood is on your hands."

My hands are already bloody, Matthias thought.

They headed back to the inn, and when they entered the common room, Matthias caught a glimpse of the innkeeper giving them a suspicious glance. He figured the man must have seen them tailing the elderly gentleman, but then he remembered that they hadn't paid for their food or lodging yet.

"My apologies," Matthias said, fishing several coins from the pocket of his cloak. He laid them on the table and added an extra one for good measure. "We were looking for a shop to get some supplies."

The innkeeper's demeanor softened as he pocketed the coins, nodding in approval. "Supplies, eh? Stocking up for a journey?"

Matthias nodded. "Yes. We have a long road ahead of us," he said vaguely, not wanting to reveal too much.

"Where are you headed?"

Matthias stared at the innkeeper as if he could discern the man's intentions. The burly man raised his hands placatingly. "I'm not trying to pry." He leaned in slightly, lowering his voice. "If I may offer a word of advice... beware the forests to the east. Rumors say they're haunted by spirits and creatures of the dark."

"Is Valen to the east?" Evelyn asked.

Matthias shot her a glare but she ignored him.

"Ah, treasure seekers," the innkeeper chuckled. "Normally I can tell by the looks of people. I'll admit I didn't have you two pegged as fortune hunters, but then again, it's been a while since I've seen any come through here. Valen is west of here, about a day's ride on horseback."

"Thank you," Matthias said. "I think we're going to retire to the room for now. We've been on the road a while."

The innkeeper shooed them off with a smile, and Matthias led the way to their room. Once inside, he latched the lock and unbuckled his sword belt.

"What are you doing?" Evelyn asked.

"I'm going to get some sleep. If you want the bed, I'll sleep on the floor."

"We don't have time to sleep! We need to get moving."

Matthias stared at her, trying to be patient. "I'm exhausted. In case you forgot, we left in the middle of the night. If I don't sleep now, we won't make it very far before I doze off."

Evelyn fumed, but she didn't say anything.

"So do you want the bed or the floor?"

6

MATTHIAS AND EVELYN TRAVELED WESTWARD on foot, unsure exactly where they needed to go. A merchant caravan was kind enough to point them in the right direction, and after traveling on the main road for roughly an hour, they departed onto an overgrown path. It was obvious the trail had once been well-trodden, but now it was swallowed by twisted roots and thick undergrowth.

Matthias pushed a low-hanging branch out of his way, his boots crunching on fallen leaves. Beside him, Evelyn walked in silence, sweat collecting on her forehead. The air around them felt heavy, and Matthias wished he'd had the foresight to bring lighter clothes.

As they pushed through the thick vegetation, the trees suddenly cleared and they found themselves in a large open field. The ruins of Valen sprawled before them. Massive stone columns, cracked and weathered by time, jutted out of the ground like jagged teeth. Walls lay in heaps of rubble, and creeping vines wound their way over every surface. Despite the decay, an eerie beauty lingered.

"I think this is it," Evelyn said.

"Doesn't look too welcoming," Matthias muttered.

"I don't think it's meant to be. If what that old man said is true, this place is probably riddled with traps. That would explain why no one ever returns."

Matthias scanned the ruins, looking for an entrance. A broken archway loomed ahead, its once intricate carvings now faint and weathered. Strange runes glowed faintly along its surface, their soft blue light barely noticeable. They advanced forward, and Evelyn stopped in front of the archway, her brow furrowed as she studied the symbols.

"Don't touch anything," Matthias warned. "It could be some sort of enchantment."

"I'm not a sorcerer, but I don't think these symbols are magical in nature." She ran a finger over one of the runes, and some of the glowing material was on her finger. "It's sticky like paint. And there's a riddle here," she said, tracing her fingers over the ancient text. Her lips moved silently as she read, her eyes narrowing in thought.

"Well?" Matthias prompted, glancing over his shoulder as if expecting the ruins themselves to rise up against them.

"Patience," Evelyn shot back, though her tone lacked its usual bite. "It says, 'Only the brave of heart and steady of mind may enter. Speak the words that open the path, and prove your worth to claim the sword of kings.'"

Matthias frowned. "And what's that supposed to mean?"

"How should I know? But at least this proves the sword is real."

"Maybe it's a phrase related to Valen? He was the first king of Midia, so that would make sense."

Evelyn shrugged. "This was your idea."

Matthias scowled at her, then wandered the ruins, looking for any clue that could help them unravel the riddle. His eyes landed on a partially crumbled statue with faded inscriptions. Since he wasn't fluent in the Midian language, he called Evelyn over to decipher the words for him.

She brushed away moss and dirt that obscured the engravings and read them aloud, "'By the will of King Valen, the land shall prosper and its people flourish. His sword, a beacon of hope in the darkest times, shall never falter.'"

Matthias pondered the words, letting them sink in. "'A beacon of hope in the darkest times'... Maybe that's the key."

Evelyn's eyes lit up with understanding. "The words that open the path... 'beacon of hope.' Try saying that to the archway."

Matthias returned to the archway and said, "Beacon of hope."

At first, nothing happened. He looked at Evelyn questioningly, and a low rumble echoed through the ruins as the ground beneath their feet trembled. The scraping of stone filled the air, and the slab in the middle of the archway slid to the side, revealing a steep staircase descending into the earth.

Matthias stared into the dark opening, second guessing his decision to seek out this place. "Why do I get the feeling this is going to be more trouble than it's worth?"

Evelyn stepped toward the opening, glancing at him over her shoulder and offering a faint smile. "You coming?"

Together, they descended into the depths. The staircase spiraled deep into the earth, the air growing warmer and mustier with each step. The faint glow of the runes along the walls was their only light, which made shadows dance on the walls.

When the staircase finally ended, they found themselves in a narrow corridor. The walls were smooth and dark, etched with the same glowing runes that had guided their way. The passage stretched forward, disappearing into the gloom. Matthias took a cautious step forward, his boots scraping against the stone. The sound echoed unnaturally.

"Wait," Evelyn said, grabbing his arm. She crouched low, her fingers brushing the ground. "Look here."

Matthias followed her gaze and saw faint markings on the floor, almost invisible in the dim light. A series of small squares were etched into the stone, arranged in a grid pattern.

"Pressure plates," Matthias murmured. "This whole corridor is probably rigged."

"What happens if we step on the wrong one?"

Matthias gave her a grim look. "Nothing good."

Evelyn pulled a small pouch from her belt and carefully removed a handful of powder. Sprinkling it lightly over the floor ahead, the markings of the pressure plates became clearer. Some squares glowed faintly in response, while others remained dull.

"Clever," Matthias said.

His pulse quickened as he took his first step. The ground beneath him felt solid, but every nerve in his body screamed that danger was near. Evelyn followed close behind, mirroring his steps.

Halfway down the corridor, Matthias's boot scuffed the edge of a glowing square. Instantly, a low grinding noise echoed through the passage. Evelyn froze, her eyes darting upward.

"Get down!" she shouted.

Matthias dropped to the ground as a volley of arrows shot from hidden slits in the walls, whizzing past where his head had been a moment before. One grazed his arm, tearing through the fabric of his sleeve and leaving a shallow cut. He hissed in pain, clutching his arm.

"Let me see it," Evelyn said.

"I'm fine," he replied, shaking off the sting of the wound. "It just took me by surprise."

They continued onward, moving slower now. As they neared the end of the corridor, Matthias's vision began to blur. He leaned against the wall, sweat trickling down his brow.

"What is it?"

Matthias's knees buckled and he slumped to the ground, narrowly missing one of the pressure plates.

"My skin is on fire," he slurred. "Something's... wrong."

7

"You've been poisoned," Evelyn said.

Matthias felt a surge of panic at her words. Poisoned? The burning sensation spread through his veins, and he struggled to stay conscious. The edges of his vision darkened, and he could feel his heartbeat pounding in his ears.

Evelyn quickly began rummaging through her pack, pulling out vials and herbs in a flurry of motion. Matthias watched her with bleary eyes, his thoughts muddled. The pain intensified, causing his muscles to spasm involuntarily. This couldn't be how he died. Evelyn produced a vial filled with a shimmering red liquid and uncorked it, carefully helping Matthias to drink a small amount.

The effects were almost immediate as the burning sensation in Matthias's veins began to subside, replaced by a cooling sensation spreading through his body.

"Is it helping?"

Matthias nodded weakly. "It's a good thing you came with me."

Evelyn's face softened with relief at his words, though worry still lingered in her eyes. "I couldn't let you go charging into danger alone," she scolded gently, her fingers brushing against his forehead to check his temperature.

Matthias managed a weak smile in response, grateful for her quick thinking and expertise. As the antidote continued to work its magic, color returned to his cheeks and strength flowed back into his limbs. He pushed himself up with Evelyn's assistance.

"Are you able to continue, or should we turn back?"

"I'm not letting a little poison stop me," Matthias replied. "Let's find that sword and get out of here."

As they neared the end of the corridor, the traps became more obvious. A section of the wall began to shift, revealing hidden blades that swiped out in a rhythmic pattern. Matthias timed his movements carefully, darting past the blades and catching Evelyn's hand to pull her through just as they retracted.

Finally, they reached the end of the passage, where a heavy stone door loomed before them. Matthias wiped a droplet of sweat from his face. "That was fun."

Evelyn shot him a sharp look. "This isn't a joke, Matthias. If we're not careful, one of us isn't walking out of here." Her tone softened as she glanced at his injured arm. "Let me check your wound."

Matthias shook his head. "We need to keep moving."

Evelyn forcefully grabbed ahold of his arm and inspected the cut. "It's not deep," she concluded after a moment, "but we need to clean and bandage it properly once we're out of here. The poison was probably the worst part, but it's best to be on the safe side."

Matthias nodded, grateful for her concern despite their volatile relationship. He turned to the door and pushed on it. It was heavy, but it swung open slowly, revealing another dark passage beyond.

Matthias exhaled heavily. "If that was the first trap, I don't want to know what's next."

The corridor beyond the door widened into a cavernous chamber, its walls glittering with embedded crystals that refracted the light of the runes into an array of shifting colors. At the center of the room stood a circular dais, its surface engraved with intricate symbols that pulsed faintly, as though alive. Surrounding the dais were five stone pillars, each bearing a unique emblem carved deeply into their surfaces.

Matthias approached cautiously, his boots echoing against the smooth stone floor. "Let me guess... another trap?"

"Not quite," Evelyn said, her eyes narrowing as she studied the room. She gestured toward the dais. "This looks like a test of wit. The early builders of Midia valued the mind as much as the body."

"How do you know so much about the people of Midia?"

Evelyn's lips quirked into a wry smile. "Let's just say I've had my fair share of adventures and acquired some useful knowledge along the way." She moved closer to the dais, examining the symbols etched into its surface with a focused gaze.

Matthias joined her, his eyes tracing the intricate patterns. "So, what do you think we're supposed to do here?"

"Five paths, five truths. Choose wrongly, and the way is barred. Choose wisely, and the light shall guide you."

The symbols on the dais flared, casting shifting patterns across the walls. Above each pillar, an ethereal light flickered, illuminating the emblems: a sword, a flame, a tree, a star, and a wave.

"What does it mean?" Matthias asked, his brow furrowing.

Evelyn pointed to the symbols on the dais. "Look closely. These markings align with the emblems on the pillars. We need to pair them correctly to proceed."

Matthias squinted at the engravings. Each one depicted a different scene: a warrior brandishing a blade, a forest set ablaze, an ocean storm, a sky full of stars, and a sapling growing in barren soil.

"So it's a matching game," Matthias said.

Evelyn nodded. "The wrong match could trigger a trap, but based on the inscriptions, it seems to imply the door will be sealed behind us."

Matthias grunted. "Locking us in here. Of course."

Evelyn crouched beside the dais, tracing her fingers over the engravings. "The symbols aren't just images; they're representations of values. Courage, destruction, renewal, guidance, and endurance. We need to think about how each emblem aligns with these."

Matthias studied the emblems again. "Courage is the sword," he said after a moment.

"That makes senses to me. Fire represents destruction, obviously. The tree could be renewal—new life growing after devastation. The star likely means guidance, and the wave could be endurance, enduring the storm."

They exchanged a glance, and Evelyn's fingers hesitated over the first symbol. "We'll need to activate these in the right order. If we're wrong…"

Matthias didn't need her to finish the sentence. His hand tightened on his sword hilt. "No pressure, then."

Evelyn touched the engraving of the sword first, then stepped back as the corresponding pillar lit with a soft glow. Nothing happened.

"Good start," Matthias said.

She moved to the flame next, pressing the engraving with a tentative hand. Again, the corresponding pillar glowed. One by one, they activated the symbols: the tree, the star, and finally the wave. When the last symbol was pressed, the chamber fell silent, the light from the pillars fading into darkness.

"Is… that supposed to happen?" Matthias asked, his voice uneasy.

Before Evelyn could answer, the dais began to sink into the floor, revealing a spiraling staircase that descended even further into the earth. The crystals on the walls dimmed, casting the room in shadow.

"It appears we passed," Evelyn said.

Matthias exhaled sharply. "Let's not celebrate just yet."

They descended the new staircase, and Matthias couldn't shake the feeling that the puzzles weren't meant to test their intellect alone—they were meant to wear them down, chipping away at their confidence.

Evelyn glanced at him as they continued into the darkness. "I suspect the next one will be harder," she said softly.

Matthias nodded, his jaw tight. "So be it."

8

THE AIR GREW THICK AND heavy as Matthias stepped into the chamber. It was smaller than the others, a circular room enclosed by walls that shimmered like liquid silver. There were no runes, no visible exits—only a suffocating silence.

"Evelyn?" Matthias called, turning to where she had been standing a moment ago.

But she was gone.

"Evelyn!" he shouted. His voice echoed back at him as though the room itself was mocking him.

He spun in place, his heart pounding. The silver walls began to ripple, distorting his reflection. Shadows coalesced, swirling around him like smoke before condensing into a solid form.

A deep voice filled the space. "You cannot hide from what lies within."

Matthias drew his sword, the blade trembling in his grip. "Show yourself!"

The shadows shifted again, morphing into a scene so vivid it made Matthias stagger back a step. He was no longer in the chamber but standing in the familiar warmth of his family's farmhouse. The scent of fresh bread and pinewood filled the air, and sunlight streamed through the windows.

For a moment, Matthias was frozen, his breath caught in his throat.

"Matthias!" His younger sister, Liana, came running toward him, her laughter echoing through the house. She was as he remembered her, her golden hair shining in the light. Behind her, his mother stood by the hearth, stirring a pot, while his father sharpened tools at the table.

"Liana?" Matthias whispered, lowering his sword.

But something was wrong. The sunlight dimmed, and the air grew cold. The laughter faded, replaced by a distant rumble like thunder. Matthias's parents turned to him, their faces pale and gaunt, their eyes hollow.

"Why didn't you save us?" his mother said, her voice brittle and cracking like dry leaves.

Matthias staggered back. "What? No… I—"

The walls of the farmhouse dissolved into smoke, revealing a battlefield drenched in blood. The screams of the dying filled the air, and dragons wheeled above, their roars shaking the earth. At the center of it all, Matthias stood, his armor slick with blood, his sword heavy in his hand.

Before him lay his wife and son, their bodies broken and lifeless.

"No!" Matthias cried, dropping to his knees. He reached for them, but the ground beneath him turned to ash, swallowing them whole.

The shadowy voice returned, circling him like a predator. "You fear failure. You fear losing those you love. You tell yourself you fight for them, but will they ever forgive the blood on your hands?"

Matthias clenched his fists, his knuckles white. "This isn't real. This is a trick!"

"Is it?" the voice taunted. "Or is it the truth you refuse to face?"

The battlefield melted away, replaced by a void of endless darkness. From the shadows stepped a figure—himself.

The doppelgänger's eyes burned with a cold, merciless light. "You can't protect them," it said, its voice an icy mirror of his own.

"Every step you take leads them closer to ruin. The more you fight, the more you destroy."

Matthias gritted his teeth, his hand tightening around his sword. "I fight to protect them. To make a better world for them."

The shadow version of himself smirked, raising its own blade. "Prove it."

The doppelgänger lunged, and Matthias barely had time to parry the strike. Their swords clashed, the sound ringing through the void like a bell. Blow after blow came, each strike forcing Matthias back.

"You're weak," the shadow spat, its movements fluid and relentless. "You'll never be enough."

Matthias's arms ached, his breath coming in ragged gasps. The shadow forced him to his knees, its blade pressing against his throat.

"Admit it," it whispered. "You'll fail them, just as you failed your brother."

Matthias froze, the words striking deeper than any blade. His mind flashed to his brother's face, the memory of that fateful day when he hadn't been fast enough, strong enough, to save him.

Tears burned in his eyes, but he shook his head. "No. I won't let the past define me. I've made mistakes, but I fight because I must. Because it's the only way to honor their memory."

With a roar, Matthias surged upward, his sword slicing through the shadow. The figure dissolved into smoke, and the oppressive darkness lifted.

The silver walls of the chamber reappeared, and Matthias found himself standing alone once more. His chest heaved, and sweat dripped from his brow.

The voice echoed one final time, softer now. "You have faced your fear and found your truth. The path is open."

The outline of a doorway appeared, faint at first, but it solidified as Matthias approached. Beyond it, he could see Evelyn slumped against the wall, her face pale.

Matthias ran to her, kneeling at her side. "Evelyn!"

Her eyes fluttered open, and she gave him a weak smile. "You made it."

"*We* made it," Matthias said, his voice firm.

He helped her to her feet, supporting her weight as they continued ahead. The passage was narrow and treacherous, carved from ancient stone that crumbled at the edges. Matthias supported Evelyn as best he could, her weight heavy against him.

"What happened to you? One moment you were there, and the next you were gone."

"I was in some sort of labyrinth, and I didn't see the trap in front of me. You vanished, and I was too focused on trying to find you. Once I realized the danger, I couldn't move quick enough to avoid the trap."

Blood seeped through the makeshift bandage wrapped around her leg. Her breathing was shallow, and her skin was turning pale. "I'll be fine," she murmured, though her voice lacked its usual strength.

"Not without help you won't be," Matthias replied firmly, his jaw tight as he scanned the dark corridor for a safe place to rest.

"I've been hurt worse." Her smile was faint, tinged with pain. "Don't stop on account of me."

Matthias ignored her protest, guiding her toward a small alcove where the floor was smooth enough to sit. The faint light of the chamber illuminated the strain in her features.

"You're staying here until I take care of that wound," he said, lowering her gently to the ground.

Evelyn gritted her teeth as he removed the bandage. The sight of the injury made Matthias's stomach turn. It was deep, and blood pooled in the gaping wound. He rifled through her supplies, pulling out a salve and fresh bandages.

"Stay still," he ordered, though his touch was gentle as he worked.

Evelyn hissed through her teeth when he applied the salve. "You're surprisingly good at this."

"Valkyra gets herself hurt more often than you'd think," Matthias replied, focusing on his task. "Dragons don't complain as much, though."

That earned him a weak chuckle. "You'd be surprised. I've heard some dragons are worse than humans."

The humor faded as Matthias tied off the bandage, and Evelyn's gaze met his. "Don't let me slow you down. If you need to leave me here—"

"No." His voice was resolute, cutting her off.

Evelyn blinked, startled by the intensity in his tone.

"I'm not abandoning you."

Evelyn's expression softened, her voice quieter. "It's not about abandoning me. It's about doing what's necessary."

"What's necessary is keeping both of us alive," Matthias said. "I'll carry you if I have to."

Evelyn studied him for a moment, her lips curving into a faint smile. "You've changed, you know."

Matthias frowned. "What do you mean?"

"You're more confident," she said, leaning back against the stone wall. "When you first came to the school, you were so wrapped up in your fears—of failing, of not being good enough. But now... I see it in the way you carry yourself, the way you make decisions. You're not the same man who walked into the Citadel."

Matthias hesitated, the weight of her words settling over him. She was right. The trials he'd faced forced him to confront parts of himself he'd tried to ignore—his doubts, his fears, his guilt. And while those feelings hadn't disappeared, he'd found something stronger beneath them: resolve.

He sighed. "Maybe I have changed. But I'm still not leaving you behind."

Evelyn nodded. "Good, because I'd hate to have to crawl after you."

Matthias smirked. After ensuring she was as comfortable as possible, he stood and adjusted his sword belt. He glanced down at her.

"Rest here. I'll scout the way ahead and make sure it's clear."

9

A CHAMBER LOOMED AHEAD, ITS massive stone doors carved with intricate patterns of griffons flying among the stars. Matthias's footsteps echoed in the corridor as he approached, his heart pounding.

Evelyn leaned on his shoulder. Her face was still pale, but the color was starting to return. Her injury slowed her pace, but it wasn't stopping her. She glanced at Matthias, her eyes sharp despite her exhaustion. "This is it."

"How do you know?"

Evelyn brushed her fingers against the weathered carvings on the doors. "It says beyond this door lies the 'power of Valen.' That must be the sword."

Matthias stared at the doors, wondering if another test awaited them inside. "It's probably been sealed for centuries," he said.

"And we'll be the first to step inside... the first to claim the sword."

Matthias steeled himself and pushed against the doors. A faint hum filled the air. The patterns on the stone began to glow, lines of light tracing the intricate carvings until the entire surface radiated a soft, silver aura. The doors groaned as they parted, revealing the chamber beyond.

The room was vast, its ceiling lost in shadow. Pillars of crystal rose from the floor, casting shimmering light across the walls. At the center stood a raised platform, and on it rested a sword.

Matthias and Evelyn approached cautiously, their footsteps muffled by the thick layer of dust coating the floor. The weapon was unlike anything Matthias had imagined. Its blade was forged from an unknown metal that shimmered with a prismatic sheen. At its head was a griffon's claw clutching an orb of swirling light.

"You found it," Evelyn whispered, her voice tinged with awe. "The sword of the first king of Midia. It's beautiful."

Matthias stared at the sword, its power almost tangible. He felt its pull, as though it recognized him, called to him. But as he reached for it, Evelyn's hand shot out, gripping his arm.

"Wait," she said, her voice sharp.

Matthias froze. "What is it?"

"There's no way this weapon is unguarded."

"What do you mean? We just passed the tests to get here. Surely there's nothing else in the way."

As if in answer to her warning, the air around them shifted. The light dimmed, and a deep rumble resonated through the chamber. Matthias instinctively stepped in front of Evelyn as a figure materialized on the platform.

It was a ghostly apparition, a man clad in shimmering armor, his eyes glowing with an otherworldly light. He held a sword identical to the one on the platform, his expression grave.

"Who dares to claim the sword?" the figure demanded, his voice echoing as though it came from the walls themselves.

Matthias squared his shoulders, meeting the figure's gaze. "I am Matthias Baines of Osnen. We seek the weapon to stop the False King."

The guardian studied him for a moment, his ethereal eyes piercing his very soul. "This blade is not meant for the unworthy. It is a burden as much as it is a gift. To wield it is to sacrifice. Do you understand this?"

Matthias hesitated, the weight of the guardian's words sinking in. "I do," he said finally. "If that's what it takes to save my people, then I will bear it."

The guardian's gaze shifted to Evelyn, his expression unreadable. "And you? Do you stand beside him willingly, knowing the dangers this path brings?"

Evelyn straightened despite her injury, her voice firm. "I do. We've come this far together, and we're not turning back now."

The guardian nodded, a flicker of approval crossing his face. "Very well. But the sword does not choose lightly. One final question remains: Are you willing to give all that you are to protect this world?"

Matthias's throat tightened. He thought of his family, his home, the lives that depended on him. And then he thought of Evelyn, wounded but unwavering.

"I am," he said. "I'll give everything if I need to."

The guardian smiled and stepped aside, gesturing to the blade. "Then it is yours. May your heart remain pure, and your will unbroken."

As the apparition faded, the chamber grew still once more. Matthias approached the platform, his fingers trembling as he reached for the sword. The moment his hand closed around the hilt, a surge of energy shot through him, filling him with warmth and light. The orb at the staff's head flared brightly, and for a moment, Matthias felt as though he could hear the heartbeat of the world itself.

Evelyn watched him, her expression a mix of curiosity and pride. "You did it."

Matthias turned to her, the sword glowing faintly in his hand. "*We* did it," he corrected.

But deep in his chest, he felt the weight of the guardian's words. The sword was his now, but it came with a price—one he knew he would have to pay.

The soft glow of the sword's orb illuminated the dim corridor as Matthias and Evelyn made their way back through the ruins of Valen. Evelyn leaned against the crumbling wall for support, her steps slower than usual. Matthias glanced at her. "How's the wound?"

"It's fine," she replied, though her voice was thin. "I'll manage."

"You don't have to," Matthias replied, shifting the sword to his other hand and offering his arm. "Let me help."

Evelyn hesitated but relented, leaning on him as they continued forward. As they neared the exit, Valkyra's presence touched Matthias's mind. It was faint due to the distance between them, but he could sense her pride at his success.

We're on our way back, Matthias told the dragon.

When they emerged into the open air, the ruins behind them seemed smaller and less foreboding. The sky was a welcome sight, and the warmth of the sun on his skin eased the tension that had settled in Matthia's bones.

They paused at the edge of the ruins to give Evelyn a moment to rest. She sat on the ground and closed her eyes.

"Are you all right?" Matthias asked.

"I will be, but I don't think I can make it back to the inn."

"I'm not leaving you here, so don't ask me to again."

"You can't carry me that far. And I wouldn't let you even if you could."

Matthias reached out to Valkyra. *I know it's risky, but I need you to come to us. Evelyn was injured and can't walk.*

I've grown bored hiding in the trees. I'm on my way.

Valkyra arrived as the sun was beginning to descend beyond the horizon. She landed among the ruins and lowered her head as Matthias approached, her eyes locking onto the sword.

So this is the weapon, she said, her mental tone curious. *It feels... ancient. Powerful.*

I'm sure it is, Matthias said, lifting the blade slightly. The sword responded, its orb glowing faintly as if acknowledging the dragon's attention.

Evelyn got up on her own, her face twisted in agony. She limped over to where Matthias was and pushed his hand away as he offered to help her. "We need to decide our next move. The False King won't stop, and now that we have this..." She gestured to the sword. "We have a way to fight him."

"Then we stop running. We take the fight to him."

Evelyn's brow furrowed. "You're serious?"

"Yes," Matthias said. "Curate Aric's instructions were to learn what we could and report back. We know what the False King is plotting, so I think we should return to the Citadel. When the Order hears what we have to say, I think they'll want to strike at him before he can strike us. And having found this weapon is an added bonus."

Valkyra rumbled her approval. Matthias placed a hand on her scales, rubbing them comfortingly. "The sun is going down now. We can wait until it's dark, and head back unseen."

Evelyn nodded. "All right. But first, let's eat something. I'm starved."

Matthias gathered some fallen branches from the woods and stacked them into a pile. Valkyra breathed her flames onto the wood, igniting a fire. They sat near the blaze and ate some of the food they'd purchased at the village.

Once night fell over the landscape, Matthias helped Evelyn climb onto Valkyra's back, then secured the sword in a sheath strapped to his saddle before climbing up and sitting behind Evelyn. The dragon spread her wings, and with a mighty leap, they took to the air, speeding toward Osnen.

10

The walls of the Citadel had never looked so imposing—or so welcoming. Valkyra landed with a graceful thud in the central courtyard, her massive wings stirring the cold morning air and scattering dust and loose stones.

Matthias dismounted first, then helped Evelyn as she slid down. She favored her injured side but masked her discomfort with practiced ease. A stable hand approached and offered to take Valkyra's reins.

"Thank you," Matthias said. "Please make sure she gets fresh meat and water."

The dragon snorted, sending a puff of warm air into the boy's face. *I'll handle myself,* Valkyra said, her tone laced with amusement. Matthias gave her an affectionate pat on the snout before retrieving the sword from her saddle.

As they made their way through the fortress, the halls of the Citadel buzzed with activity. Clerks hurried with stacks of parchment, and riders rushed about on various tasks, their expressions serious. It was as if war was imminent.

"What did we miss?" Evelyn asked.

"Your guess is as good as mine."

Matthias escorted Evelyn to the infirmary, then made his way to Curate Aric's office. Inside, Curate Aric stood at the head of a long table, its surface plastered with parchments and maps. His piercing eyes locked onto Matthias immediately, then flicked to the glowing sword in his hands.

"You've returned," Aric said. "Where's Evelyn?"

"She's in the infirmary. She'll be fine," he added as Aric's expression darkened. "She was injured but not by an enemy."

"I see. What's that?" he nodded toward the sword.

"If my information is correct, it's the only weapon that can stop the False King. We found it in the ruins of a place called Valen, but not without cost."

"Did you learn anything of Valerius's plans?"

"Yes. He's trying to craft a spell that will enslave dragons to do his bidding. He intends to invade Osnen and turn our dragons against us."

"How credible is this information?" Aric asked.

"The same person told me about this sword, and he was right. He was a servant who escaped Araphel."

Aric nodded. "I'll need to speak with Master Pevus about this. It doesn't bode well."

"If I may speak freely?"

"Of course."

"The time for defense has passed. We should strike at Midia with everything we have, take the fight to him and overwhelm his forces. If he manages to pull off that spell..." Matthias trailed off.

"I agree that we need to take action, but that's a decision for the council to make. I'll make your concerns known. Get some rest. You've earned it."

Matthias bowed his head and turned to leave.

"Leave the sword on the table," Aric said. "I want to make sure there's nothing about it that's going to work against us."

"As you command." Matthias set the sword on the table and left the room. He made his way to the infirmary to check on Evelyn, who was sitting up in bed as a healer tended to her leg. Her eyes met his, and she smiled.

"Hey," she said softly.

"Hey yourself," Matthias replied. "How are you feeling?"

"Better now that I'm not on my feet," Evelyn said with a wry smile. "Did you talk to Aric?"

"I did. He's going to share everything with the council. I was thinking of attending the meeting if you want to join me?"

Evelyn nodded.

"Good. I'll come get you before it starts. I'm going to try to sleep a little. You should do the same."

—

The council chamber was crowded with senior riders, Curates, and Master Pevus. It was warm and stuffy, and Matthias found the atmosphere suffocating. Evelyn sat at his side in a chair, her fatigue visible on her face. He was surprised she decided to attend the meeting.

Master Pevus surveyed the room with a sharp gaze. He was older, with gray hair and a beard to match. His years were etched into his face as deep lines, but his voice held the unyielding authority of a man who had carried Osnen through countless crises.

"We have heard Matthias's report," he began, his voice echoing off the chamber's walls. "Valerius, or the False King as he has come to be known, grows bolder. His dark magic threatens not only our people but the very balance of the world. If he succeeds in enslaving our dragons, Osnen will fall."

Murmurs broke out among the council members. Some argued in hushed tones, while others nodded grimly.

"Master," one of the Curates spoke up, his voice hesitant, "you speak of war, but the risks are great. To engage the enemy on his own soil could lead to great losses. Are we certain this is the best course of action?"

"That is a fair question, and one I have considered myself. Battling Midia's forces, whether here or there, will result in deaths that cannot be avoided. I believe launching an attack while Valerius is ill prepared will result in the least loss of life."

Another council member, a woman with streaks of gray in her auburn hair, leaned forward. "And what of our dragons? Will they be safe? If even one turns against us mid-battle, it could spell disaster."

"As far as we are aware, Valerius has not succeeded in taking control of a dragon," Master Pevus said. "The longer we wait heightens the chance that he'll succeed."

Curate Aric nodded, his expression grave. "You are right. Delay will cost us everything. The time has come to act. This council must decide: do we march into Midia and strike at the heart of this threat, or do we wait and risk annihilation?"

The chamber was silent for a long moment as the weight of the decision settled over everyone.

"I say we fight," Curate Anesko said.

Others nodded their agreement.

"We've been defending our borders for years, always reacting. It's time we take the fight to them," another Curate chimed in.

"All in favor?" Curate Aric asked.

Almost every hand rose.

"Then it is decided," Master Pevus declared. "The Dragon Guard will go to war. Every able-bodied rider must prepare. I will send word to the king."

11

THE CITADEL BUZZED WITH ACTIVITY as the riders mobilized for the coming assault. The courtyard, which had been silent in the early dawn, now rang with the clang of hammers striking steel and the hurried shouts of soldiers preparing for battle. Rows of dragons lined the training grounds, their scales glinting in the rising sun as their riders fastened armor to their massive frames. The air was thick with the mingling scents of leather, oil, and dragon musk.

In less than two full days, every rider had been recalled from across Osnen. Matthias stood amidst the flurry of activity, his gaze fixed on Valkyra as she was being measured by a blacksmith.

I don't need this flimsy metal, Valkyra grumbled. *It weighs me down.*

It's for added protection, Matthias replied.

The dragon didn't complain further, but he could sense her displeasure through the bond as the smith and his assistants began fitting the armor on her.

With war looming, his thoughts turned to his wife and son. He wished he could see them before he left, but there wasn't time. They would be departing shortly, and Matthias knew he had to focus on the task at hand. He had a duty to protect his home and loved ones, even if it meant risking his life in battle.

He was pulled from his thoughts when Evelyn approached. "Have you eaten yet?" she asked.

Matthias shook his head. "I will. Later."

"You said that an hour ago." Evelyn's tone was light, but her eyes betrayed her concern.

"I've had a lot to do. I still have to check Valkyra's harness."

"Master Pevus is leading this endeavor, and he found time to eat." She nodded toward the main gates where he and the Curates were gathered.

He opened his mouth to argue but stopped when Valkyra's voice brushed against his mind. *She's right, you know. If you fall from exhaustion, you are no good to anyone.*

Matthias chuckled softly, shaking his head. "Even my dragon's against me now."

"Not against you," Evelyn said, her smile growing. "With you. Always."

The moment of levity was interrupted by Curate Aric's voice announcing they were departing soon.

"I wish I could go with you," Evelyn lamented. "I know I'm not a warrior, but my skills as a healer would be put to good use."

"You need to rest and let your leg heal. Besides, those who are injured will be returning here. You'll still be of help."

"Are you ready? For the battle, I mean."

"I don't think anyone can truly be ready for what's coming," Matthias admitted.

"You've proven yourself time and again. Trust in that. And trust in those who fight alongside you."

"I will. I'll see you when we return." Matthias made his way to Valkyra's side. The dragon stood tall, her blue scales gleaming like polished sapphires. He checked her saddle, which had been reinforced with additional straps to accommodate the armor.

Are you ready? Matthias ran a hand along Valkyra's snout.

I'm always ready.

Evelyn joined them and handed Matthias a wrapped package. "Here. Bread and dried meat. No excuses this time."

Matthias smirked but took the food. "Thanks."

As he ate a brief meal, the sounds of the Citadel's preparations filled the air. It was a symphony of war, and every note carried the weight of what lay ahead.

When the time came, Matthias climbed onto Valkyra's back, adjusting his position in the saddle. Valkyra spread her wings, the powerful muscles rippling beneath her scales, and with a mighty leap, she joined the other dragons taking to the sky. A chorus of roars erupted from the beasts, and Matthias felt a chill of excitement run through him. They soared beyond the Citadel, their formation heading north to Midia.

Matthias leaned forward on Valkyra's back, his gaze fixed on the horizon. The lead dragon, a massive green beast ridden by Master Pevus, directed the formation's movements. As the border came in sight, Matthias could see faint glimmers of light scattered across the mountainside— Midian outposts.

Those are new, he told Valkyra.

Curate Aric's voice echoed within his mind, amplified by the magical link shared by all dragon riders. *Do not engage unless ordered. Our goal is to cross unnoticed.*

The dragons shifted into a tighter formation, their powerful wings beating in unison as they passed the mountain. Matthias's pulse quickened as they slipped past the watchfires, their shadows fleeting and ghostlike. He clenched Valkyra's reins, every muscle in his body taut as he awaited the inevitable—an arrow, a battle cry, a horn blasting a warning.

But nothing happened.

As they crossed over a valley, the watchfires faded into the distance. The Dragon Guard had successfully crossed into Midian territory. The terrain below shifted from rugged peaks to rolling hills, and Matthias breathed easier.

That felt too easy.

Maybe they let us in, Valkyra replied.

Why would they do that?

They want us here.

Or they are afraid to stop us, Matthias said, though his tone carried little conviction.

As they pressed deeper into Midia, the hills gave way to desolate plains, the soil cracked and barren. Ahead, a black mountain rose from the earth like a shadow. Matthias knew Araphel was built upon the top of an extinct volcano, but seeing it in person sent a shiver down his spine. The dark fortress loomed ominously, its spires reaching for the sky like jagged claws. Around its base, a sprawling camp bustled with activity—Midian soldiers drilling in formation, tents pitched in neat rows, and siege weapons being readied.

Matthias's heart hammered in his chest as he took in the sheer scale of Valerius's forces. This was no mere outpost; it was a stronghold, a bastion of darkness that threatened to consume the land.

Prepare for battle, Curate Aric's voice echoed.

The dragons banked and began their descent just as a bell tower began clanging. The courtyard of the fortress erupted into chaos, and griffons took to the air.

They know we're here, Valkyra said.

Matthias unstrapped his crossbow from the saddle. There was no turning back now.

12

THE SKY BECAME A WHIRLWIND of disorder. Dragons and griffons collided in brutal aerial combat, their roars and shrieks blending into a cacophony of sound. The clash was fierce. Fire spewed from open jaws, painting the sky in a kaleidoscope of destruction.

Hold on! Valkyra shouted as she dove toward an oncoming griffon rider. She unleashed a torrent of flames, and the griffon shrieked in pain, its rider flailing before tumbling from the saddle.

Matthias raised his crossbow and fired, the bolt piercing another rider in the shoulder. His griffon faltered, veering away from the fight. Valkyra darted through the fray, dodging strikes and returning them with precision. The battle blurred into a series of moments—fire and steel, cries of triumph and pain.

Below in the courtyard, a robed figure raised a staff, releasing a pulse of dark magic that surged outward. The effect was immediate and devastating. Some of the dragons hesitated, their movements erratic. Others turned on their riders, their eyes glowing with an unnatural green light.

Matthias's heart sank as he watched one of his comrades struggle against their own dragon, the beast snapping and snarling as if possessed. Dread coiled around him as he considered how to fend off Valkyra.

Is the spell affecting you?

No, Valkyra replied. *Others are not so fortunate.*

Even from a distance, Matthias could feel the oppressive weight of the magic, a malevolent force that seemed to drain the very air of life.

We have to stop him! Matthias yelled.

I agree, but that's easier said than done.

The figure in the courtyard continued his spell, the dark magic spreading like a plague.

We need to confront him directly.

Breaking through the enemy lines is no small feat, Valkyra argued.

We will fight our way to him.

Valkyra rumbled, her concerns flowing through the bond. *You'll need the sword. Who has it?*

Before Matthias could reply, he watched in horror as a group of griffons attacked Curate Aric, overwhelming his dragon.

He does, Matthias said.

Valkyra's powerful wings beat against the air as she cut through the chaos of battle toward the endangered Curate. The wind whipped past them as they closed in on the griffons, who were focused solely on their target. With a mighty roar, Valkyra breathed a stream of scorching flames at the lead griffon, causing it to veer off course with a piercing screech. Matthias seized the opportunity and leaned forward, firing his crossbow. The bolt found its mark and punched a hole through a second griffon's wing.

Aric's dragon fought valiantly, deflecting strikes and unleashing bursts of flame, but the griffons were relentless, their talons slashing and beaks snapping. Valkyra angled sharply, snatching a griffon up in one claw while she whipped her tail into another.

"The sword!" Matthias shouted at Curate Aric. "Where's the sword?"

Aric pulled the blade from the saddle and attempted to hurl it, but his dragon jerked away from a strike and the sword went flying askew, twirling downward end over end. Valkyra dove after the weapon.

Below, the robed figure with the staff retreated inside the castle. The ground quaked, and shadows writhed like living things. The roar of battle faltered as confusion spread through the Osnen ranks. Some dragons froze mid-flight, their wings folding awkwardly as they spiraled toward the ground. Others turned on their riders, their eyes blazing with a sickly green glow.

A squadron of dragons began tearing into one another, their massive bodies thrashing as their riders screamed in vain, struggling to regain control.

It's spreading, Matthias said, his voice tight with dread. His focus turned to Valkyra. *Are you still with me?*

For now... the pressure is growing.

Matthias could hear the strain in her voice. Their bond was growing thin, disintegrating under the magic. The wind roared as Valkyra tucked her wings close to her body, cutting through the air at impossible speed to reach the sword.

The weapon struck the ground point first, embedding itself in the earth. Valkyra didn't let up, and Matthias realized her body had gone limp.

Valkyra! he screamed. *Valkyra!*

She struck the ground hard, sending up a spray of earth and debris. Matthias was flung from the saddle, rolling across the unforgiving terrain until he came to a stop. Pain exploded through him, every nerve and muscle screaming in protest. He lay there in shock, staring up at the chaos unfolding in the sky.

The battle had devolved into madness. The magic continued to spread, infecting everything it touched. Matthias's heart seized with fear for Valkyra. He staggered to his feet, ignoring the pain that flared in his limbs. His vision blurred as he staggered toward his dragon.

She lay motionless on the ground, her powerful wings splayed out at odd angles. Desperation clawed at his chest as he rushed to her side and dropped to his knees beside her. His hands shook as he reached out to touch her side. No warmth greeted him, no reassuring hum of life beneath his fingers.

"Valkyra," he whispered aloud, his eyes full of tears. "Please, don't leave me."

He choked with grief. The battle continued to rage around him, but Matthias felt as if the world had shrunk to encompass only him and his fallen companion. Tears streamed down his cheeks as he cradled Valkyra's massive head in his lap, her eyes fixed and unseeing.

"I failed you."

Matthias bowed his head and wept, the weight of defeat pressing down on him with unbearable force. He had lost not only a companion but a friend. Their bond had transcended mere words, and the enormity of Valkyra's death settled over him like a heavy shroud.

The echo of Aric's voice cut through his despair.

Riders, to me!

Matthias looked up and saw Curate Aric rallying those whose dragons had not succumbed to the dark magic. He stood as a beacon of hope against the darkness. Matthias's grief burned away as rage took its place.

He staggered to his feet, the pain in his body forgotten. Without Valkyra by his side, he would have to find another way to confront the enemy. He looked around for the sword of Valen, his eyes landing on the blade buried in the earth not far from where Valkyra lay.

Matthias strode to it and wrenched it from the ground. Each step was a battle against the grief threatening to consume him, but he pushed it down, burying it as deep as he could. He turned his gaze to the fortress of Araphel and clenched his jaw.

He was going to kill the False King.

THE FORTRESS LOOMED LIKE A monstrous beast against the darkening sky. From this distance, the cries of battle and the clash of steel faded into a dull roar, leaving Matthias in a bubble of silence broken only by the wind.

The gates had been shattered in the earlier assault, twisted and hanging from their hinges like the ribs of some long-dead beast. He stepped cautiously inside, his boots crunching against the debris littering the entryway. The stench of sulfur and decay greeted him, a reminder of the foul magic that ravaged the sky.

The courtyard was eerily quiet, the only sound the faint crackle of distant flames and the occasional rumble as the ground trembled, the result of a dragon falling from the sky. Shadows seemed to writhe along the walls, unnatural in their movements.

The shadows thickened as he entered the fortress, and a chill ran down his spine. Whispered voices began to fill the air, faint at first but growing louder with each step.

"Matthias…"

He froze. The voice was unmistakable—his wife's.

"How could you abandon us?"

His throat tightened, but he forced himself to move forward. The whispers twisted, becoming his son's voice, then Valkyra's, all accusing him of failure.

"You'll fail them, just as you failed us," the voices hissed.

"Enough!" Matthias shouted, the sword flaring with light.

The shadows recoiled, retreating to the edges of the hall. The whispers faded, replaced by an oppressive silence. Matthias pressed on, his heart pounding in his chest. He could feel the fortress itself resisting his presence, as if the False King's magic had made the very stones hostile to intruders.

At last, he reached a massive set of double doors, their surfaces engraved with runes that pulsed faintly with malevolent energy. Matthias took a deep breath and placed a hand on the doors. With a powerful push, they swung open, revealing the shadowed throne room beyond.

It was a cavernous expanse, its walls draped in shadows cast by the flickering light of braziers. The air was humid and thick with the acrid tang of something he couldn't quite place, making each breath a struggle. At the far end of the room, the False King sat upon a throne of black stone, its jagged edges seemingly carved from the bones of some creature.

He rose as Matthias entered, his long cloak trailing behind him like a shadow come to life. Valerius Draven was tall and hearty, his body covered in dark armor etched with runes that glowed with a red tinge. His eyes burned with malevolence, twin orbs of cold fire that pierced the dimness of the room.

"What do we have here?" Valerius said, his voice booming. "Someone with a death wish?"

Matthias stepped forward, the sword of Valen pulsing with a light that seemed to push back against the oppressive darkness. "I've come to end your reign of terror. Free the dragons from your vile magic."

Valerius laughed, a hollow sound that chilled Matthias to the core. "Free them? They are mine, bound by powers far greater than your pitiful blade. Do you think a relic of a forgotten age will save you?"

"You *will* release them," Matthias replied, his voice firm despite the fear coiling in his chest.

"Let us see if you are worthy of the blade you wield."

Valerius raised his hand, and tendrils of shadow snaked across the floor toward Matthias, whipping toward him with the speed of striking vipers. He sidestepped the first and brought the sword down on the second, its light severing the shadowy appendage with a hiss.

Matthias charged, his blade aimed at the Valeriu's heart, but the man unsheathed his own sword and unleashed a torrent of green fire from the tip of the blade. Matthias raised weapon just in time, its light creating a shimmering shield that absorbed the flames.

"Impressive," Valerius sneered. "But I cannot be bested by brute force."

He stabbed his sword into the ground, and the throne room shifted. The floor cracked and splintered, sending jagged pillars of stone shooting up around Matthias, cutting off his path. The shadows moved again, forming spectral figures that lunged at him with ethereal weapons.

Matthias spun, cutting through the phantoms as they charged. Each swing of the blade sent arcs of light through the room, momentarily dispelling the darkness. But for every phantom he struck down, another took its place.

Valerius advanced slowly, his sword radiating energy. "Do you see now? You cannot win. My power is endless, my will unbreakable."

Matthias's breath came in ragged gasps as he fought, his arms burning with exertion. The room seemed to close in around him, the oppressive weight threatening to crush his resolve.

"Do you feel it yet?" Valerius taunted, his voice echoing from every corner of the room. "The weight of despair? The futility of your struggle?"

The sword flared, and he suddenly remembered the trials of Valen—the fear he had faced, the lessons he had learned. He was not the man who had entered those ruins, uncertain and afraid. He was stronger now.

Matthias steadied his stance and surged forward, weaving through the onslaught of shadowy tendrils and lunging at Valerius.

The usurper deflected the attack with his sword, the clash of light and dark sending shockwaves through the chamber.

"You may be powerful," Matthias said, his voice rising above the din, "but you are not invincible."

Valerius snarled, stabbing his sword into the ground again, sending out a wave of sickly green energy that struck Matthias square in the chest. He was hurled backward, landing hard on the cold, cracked floor. The sword of Valen skittered out of his grip, its glow dimming as it spun away.

"You cannot win," the False King hissed, his voice layered with an unnatural echo. "You believe you can because that is the delusion of hope. I will crush it from you, and from anyone else who stands in my way."

The room darkened further until Matthias couldn't see the walls or ceiling, only an endless void. Shadows coiled and shifted, forming into vague shapes that gradually became clearer. Matthias froze as he recognized the figures before him. His loved ones—his wife, son, and Valkyra—stood in a circle of pale light. Their faces were drawn with fear, their bodies frail and trembling. Behind them loomed monstrous shapes, their shadows reaching out to engulf them.

"Matthias," his wife called out, her voice small and trembling. "Help us!"

Matthias tried to rise, but his legs felt as though they were weighed down by iron chains. The shadows moved closer to his family, their twisted forms laughing with cruel, echoing voices.

"You couldn't save your dragon," Valerius's voice sneered, reverberating through the void. "You'll fail your family, too. No matter how strong you think you are, you can't protect anyone. Like everyone else, you will run from my flames."

Matthias clenched his fists. The image of Valkyra's lifeless body lying on the ground overwhelmed him with a sense of helplessness. The shadows swirled faster, their claws inches from his son's shoulder. Matthias's heart thundered in his chest as doubt clawed at him. But then, through the cacophony of voices, another memory surfaced: Evelyn's voice as she spoke to him before he left the Citadel.

"You are more than your fears, Matthias. You've faced them before, and you've risen stronger every time."

The words lit a spark in his mind, and he remembered every challenge he'd overcome, every trial that had brought him to this moment. He had survived. He had endured. And now, he had the power to make a difference.

The chains holding him down shattered as Matthias forced himself to his feet. The sword of Valen, lying a few feet away, began to glow stronger as if responding to his determination.

"You're wrong," Matthias said. "I'm not a man who runs from the flames. I'm the man who stands against them."

The shadows hesitated, their laughter faltering.

Matthias strode toward the sword, each step dispelling the darkness around him. He grabbed it off the ground, its light flaring to life and banishing the remaining shadows. The figures of his family dissolved into wisps of light, their faces calm and unburdened. The void receded, replaced by the cracked stone floor of the throne room.

Valerius stood at the far end of the room, his eyes narrowing in fury. "You think a spark of courage will save you?" he spat.

Matthias raised the sword of Valen, its glow unwavering. "It already has."

Valerius raised his sword, the dark energy gathering once more. But this time, Matthias stood tall, the light of his own blade casting away the shadows with every step forward. He was no longer weighed down by fear. He was ready to face the darkness head-on, no matter the cost.

Matthias charged, and the two met in the center of the room, steel and magic colliding. Matthias ducked under a sweep of Valerius's sword and swung his blade upward, forcing him to stumble back.

Valerius lashed out with a bolt of raw magic, striking Matthias's shoulder. Searing agony shot through his body. He staggered back, clenching his jaw against the pain. His grip on the sword tightened, and he pushed forward, each step fueled by the thought of those he sought to protect.

With the last of his strength, Matthias lunged. Valerius raised his blade to block the strike, but Matthias's sword shattered it in two. The False King screamed, the sound inhuman and filled with rage. His dark magic lashed out uncontrollably, tearing apart the room around them.

Matthias took advantage of the moment, driving his blade straight into Valerius's stomach. The blade sank deep, its light exploding outward. The False King's scream turned to a gurgle as the dark magic surrounding him began to dissolve.

"You... cannot... stop me..." Valerius rasped, his eyes wide with fury and disbelief. "Even in death, the darkness will rise again..."

Matthias twisted the blade, silencing him.

Valerius's body sank to the floor. Matthias stood over him, chest heaving. The sword still glowed faintly in his grip, but its light dimmed with the threat gone. Around him, the fortress began to tremble violently. The walls cracked, and pieces of the ceiling began to rain down. Dust billowed into the air, thickening until it stung his eyes and clawed at his throat.

He turned toward the exit but froze when he saw the destruction unfolding. An enormous slab of stone broke free, slamming into the floor and cutting off his path. Without warning, the floor gave way, crumbling like dry bread underfoot. Matthias threw himself forward, rolling as the ground splintered and swallowed itself behind him.

He rose to his knees and looked for another way out, but it was too late. The entire room was collapsing in on itself. Crawling to where the exit was, his hands scrambled against the cold stones, pushing, pulling, searching for a weakness, but the rocks did not yield, and the fortress continued its relentless descent into ruin.

His gaze swept the ruins, and there, he glimpsed a faint glimmer of hope—a narrow crevice, barely wide enough to squeeze through. He scrambled into the gap, contorting his body to fit inside the slender opening. The stones pressed close, threatening to crush him with their weight.

Matthias grunted, muscles straining against the unyielding stone. Darkness clawed at his vision, but Matthias pushed onward, driven by the thought of open skies and the chance to breathe.

Yet, as he wriggled desperately, the rocks above shifted, sealing shut the sliver of escape. Matthias froze. He was trapped—truly trapped. The tremors ceased, leaving behind a dreadful stillness. As the last of the sound faded, so too did the strength from his limbs.

The fortress, with its dying breath, had claimed him as its own.

14

THE FIRST OF THE SURVIVING riders arrived at the Citadel, their heads low and their dragons weak with exhaustion. The setting sun cast a golden glow over the courtyard, a sharp contrast to the soot-stained armor and battle-worn expressions of those returning.

Evelyn pushed through the crowd, desperate for a glimpse of Matthias's tall frame or the gleam of Valkyra's blue scales. When the final dragon landed, she realized Matthias was not among them.

The crowd that was gathered in the square erupted into cheers. The noise grated against Evelyn's ears, a cruel mockery of the loss that hung like a shroud over the survivors. There were many missing dragons, and many more saddles empty of familiar faces.

Master Pevus strode to the front of the crowd with deliberate slowness, his presence commanding instant attention. He raised his hands, calling for silence. The cheering ceased, replaced by a tense hush. All eyes turned to him.

"This day," Pevus began, his tone heavy with sorrow, "is one of both triumph and tragedy. We have won the battle. Valerius Draven, the False King, has fallen, and his dark reign has ended. For that, we must give thanks to the bravery of the Dragon Guard, the valor of our dragons, and the sacrifices of those who fought by our side."

His words hung in the air.

"But this triumph did not come without a price," he continued, his voice breaking slightly. "We have lost many of our own—friends, comrades, family. And among those fallen is Matthias Baines, the one who struck the final blow against the False King."

A ripple of shock spread through the crowd. Gasps and murmurs echoed off the stone walls, and Evelyn felt the air leave her lungs.

"Matthias," Pevus said, his voice steady once more, "gave his life to free our dragons and end the False King's dark magic. He stood alone in the heart of the enemy's fortress, knowing full well the cost of his actions. He died so that we might live, and so that our kingdom would remain free."

Tears blurred Evelyn's vision as she turned away, unable to bear the words any longer.

"Let his name be remembered," Pevus declared, his voice rising with conviction. "Let it be sung in every hall, in every home. Let our children and their children know the courage of Matthias. He died a hero, and his sacrifice will live on in the hearts of all who fight for freedom. As we celebrate this victory, let us also mourn those we have lost. Let us carry their memory with us, not as a burden but as a guiding light. Their sacrifice was not in vain. We live because of them. Osnen stands because of them."

A solemn silence settled over the courtyard. No cheers followed this speech, only the sound of the wind whispering through the battlements. Evelyn turned and pushed her way through the crowd, her chest tightening with each step.

When she finally broke free of the throng, she stumbled into the shadows of the lower courtyard, her legs trembling. The weight of grief pressed down on her, threatening to crush her entirely. She bit her lip until it bled, trying to stifle the sobs that clawed their way up her throat, but it was no use. Matthias was gone. And the world, despite their victory, felt unbearably empty without him.

—

The late afternoon sun bathed the Citadel as Curate Aric prepared for his journey. He stood in the armory, his hands methodically checking his travel gear. His dark blue robes, embroidered with silver threads that marked his station, had been freshly cleaned, though a faint crease in the fabric hinted at the tension he carried.

On the table before him lay a scroll, sealed with the royal crest of Osnen. The words within carried the weight of a kingdom's gratitude: a declaration granting Matthias and his family the title of Noble by Deed, elevating his name to one that would be remembered for generations to come.

Aric's fingers hovered over the scroll, his chest tight. He had delivered grim news many times in his role, but this task felt heavier than any before. He would not only be informing a widow of her husband's heroic death but also placing the burden of his legacy upon her and their child.

A knock at the door drew his attention. Master Pevus entered, his expression solemn. "Do you want me to come with you?"

Aric shook his head. "This is something I must do alone."

Master Pevus nodded, though his eyes betrayed his concern. "The roads are quiet for now, but take care. Valerius may be dead, but his followers won't vanish overnight."

"I'll be careful," Aric assured him. He secured the scroll in a leather case and slung it over his shoulder. After exchanging a brief clasp of hands with Master Pevus, he left the armory and made his way to the stables.

His horse, a sturdy bay mare named Lyria, was already saddled and waiting. The stablemaster handed him the reins with a quiet word of encouragement, and Aric mounted smoothly. He glanced back at the Citadel, its spires glinting in the sunlight, before urging Lyria into a steady trot.

The journey to Matthias's home was long, the path winding through rolling hills and dense forests. Aric's mind wandered as he rode, the rhythmic clip of hooves on the dirt road offering a strange solace. He thought of Matthias—the man who had stood tall against impossible odds.

By the time Aric reached the outskirts of Matthias's village, the sun was dipping below the horizon, painting the sky in hues of orange and crimson. Smoke rose lazily from chimneys, and the faint sound of children's laughter carried on the breeze.

The Baines' house was modest but well-kept, nestled at the edge of the village with a small garden out front. Aric dismounted and tied Lyria to a post, taking a moment to steady himself before approaching the door. He adjusted the leather strap of his satchel, which contained Matthias's personal effects to be returned.

Inhaling a deep breath, he knocked gently, the sound echoing in the quiet evening. Moments later, the door opened, and Matthias's wife, Lena, appeared. Her dark hair was tied back, and her face, though marked by lines of hard work, carried a quiet strength.

"Curate Aric," she greeted, her tone polite but curious. "What brings you here?"

"May I come in?" Aric asked softly.

Lena stepped aside, ushering him in. A small table sat in the center of the room, and the scent of stew lingered in the air. A boy of no more than eight years old—Eldwin, Matthias's son—peered at Aric from behind a chair, his wide eyes filled with curiosity.

Aric removed the scroll case from his shoulder, cradling it in his hands as he turned to Lena. "I bring news," he began, his voice steady despite the ache in his chest. "Matthias... he fought bravely. He gave his life to save us all and to ensure the False King's reign would end."

Lena's breath caught, her hand flying to her mouth. Her knees buckled, and she collapsed into a nearby chair. Aric knelt before her, setting the case on the table and placing a reassuring hand on hers.

"I am so sorry for your loss," he said. "But know this—Matthias died a hero. He gave his life to protect Osnen, to protect you and your son."

Tears streamed down Lena's face, but she managed a trembling nod. Eldwin stepped forward, his small hands clutching the back of the chair for support. His expression was a mix of confusion and dawning realization.

Aric opened the case and withdrew the scroll, handing it to Lena. "This is a declaration from the king," he explained. "In recognition of Matthias's bravery and sacrifice, your family has been granted the title of Noble by Deed. You and Eldwin are now part of Osnen's nobility."

Lena accepted the scroll with trembling hands, her eyes scanning the elegant script. "He... he always wanted to do something meaningful," she whispered. "And he did."

Aric rose to his feet, his gaze shifting to Eldwin. "Your father was a great man," he said. "You should be proud of him."

Eldwin met Aric's eyes, his small fists clenched at his sides. "I am," he replied, his voice quiet. "And one day, I'll be a dragon rider like him. I'll... I'll be brave like him."

A lump formed in Aric's throat, but he managed a nod. "I believe you will, Eldwin."

He turned back to Lena, inclining his head respectfully. "If you ever need anything, the Citadel will always be here for you."

Lena managed a weak smile through her tears. "Thank you, Curate."

Aric stepped outside, the cool evening air filling his lungs. He mounted Lyria and took one last look at the house before urging her into a trot. As he rode away, he couldn't shake the image of Eldwin's determined face.

"Matthias," he murmured under his breath, "your legacy will live on—in more ways than one."

15

The sun dipped below the horizon, leaving the small house in shadows. Inside, the room was silent except for the soft crackling of the fire in the hearth. Lena sat at the table, the royal scroll clutched in her trembling hands. Her tears had dried, leaving faint streaks on her cheeks, but her eyes remained fixed on the words that declared her husband a hero of Osnen.

Eldwin stood near the door, staring out at the fading light of the evening. His young face, usually bright with curiosity, was now etched with a maturity far beyond his years. His small hands were clenched into fists at his sides, his knuckles white.

He could still hear Curate Aric's words echoing in his mind: *"Your father was a great man."*

His father. Gone.

Eldwin closed his eyes, a lump rising in his throat. He had always thought of his father as invincible—a man who could do anything, who could protect them from any danger. Now, the realization of his father's sacrifice weighed heavily on him, filling his chest with a mixture of pride and unbearable grief.

He turned back to his mother, who sat silently, lost in her thoughts. The scroll lay open on the table, the flickering firelight dancing across the royal crest at the top. Eldwin stepped closer, his gaze fixed on the parchment.

"Mother," he said, his voice soft but steady.

Lena looked up, startled out of her reverie. Her red-rimmed eyes met her son's, and she managed a weak smile. "Yes, my love?"

Eldwin hesitated for a moment, his small frame trembling. But then he straightened his back, his youthful determination shining through.

"I'm going to be a dragon rider," he declared, his voice firm.

For a moment, she didn't respond. She opened her mouth to speak, to tell him that he was too young, that it was too dangerous, but the look in his eyes stopped her. He wasn't a child making an impulsive decision. He was her son, Matthias's son, and the conviction in his gaze reminded her so much of her husband that it took her breath away.

"You are?" she asked softly, her voice breaking.

Eldwin nodded, stepping closer to the table. He reached out and placed his hand on the scroll, his small fingers brushing against the words that honored his father's sacrifice.

"I'll train. I'll do whatever it takes," he continued, his voice growing stronger with each word. "I'll make him proud. I'll make both of you proud."

Lena's heart ached as she watched him, torn between wanting to protect him and knowing that she couldn't hold him back. She reached out and pulled him into her arms, holding him tightly.

"You already make me proud, my sweet boy," she whispered into his hair.

Eldwin hugged her back, his resolve hardening. When she finally released him, he stepped back, his eyes shining with unshed tears.

"I'll be the best dragon rider Osnen has ever seen," he vowed. "And I'll make sure everyone remembers what father did—for all of us."

Lena nodded, her throat too tight to speak. She watched as her son turned and walked to the door, standing in its frame as he gazed out at the evening sky.

Above, the first stars began to appear, twinkling faintly against the deep indigo. Eldwin tilted his head back, his eyes searching the heavens as though seeking his father's spirit among the constellations.

"I promise, father," he whispered, his words carried away by the evening breeze. "I'll honor your name. I'll make you proud."

And with that, the boy who had lost his father began to forge a path that would ensure Matthias's legacy lived on, not just in the songs of the people but also in his heart.

THE END

ABOUT THE AUTHOR

Hey there!

I write fantasy and space opera, and you can find all my books in many different ebook stores. You can check out my website for more information about my books, my next projects, and events I'll be attending.

If you enjoyed this book, I'd love your feedback in the form of a review on Amazon or Goodreads.

Thanks for reading!

-Richard

Website: www.richardfierce.com

Facebook: www.facebook.com/dragonfirepress